Belle

"Once upon a time"
is timeless with these retold tales:

Belle

CAMERON DOKEY

Simon Pulse

NEW YORK   LONDON   TORONTO   SYDNEY   NEW DELHI

To Jim, as they all have been,

once upon a time and always

SIMON PULSE

An imprint of Simon & Schuster Children's Publishing Division

1230 Avenue of the Americas, New York, New York 10020

This Simon Pulse paperback edition February 2017

Text copyright © 2008 by Cameron Dokey

Cover photograph copyright © 2017 by Getty Images

All rights reserved, including the right of reproduction in whole or in part in any form.

SIMON PULSE and colophon are registered trademarks of Simon & Schuster, Inc.

For information about special discounts for bulk purchases, please contact Simon & Schuster

Special Sales at 1-866-506-1949 or business@simonandschuster.com.

The Simon & Schuster Speakers Bureau can bring authors to your live event.

For more information or to book an event contact the Simon & Schuster Speakers Bureau

at 1-866-248-3049 or visit our website at www.simonspeakers.com.

Cover designed by Karina Granda

Interior designed by Mike Rosamilia

The text of this book was set in Bembo.

Manufactured in the United States of America

2 4 6 8 10 9 7 5 3

Library of Congress Control Number 2008928645

ISBN 978-1-4814-7966-0 (pbk)

ISBN 978-1-4424-3019-8 (eBook)

One

I'VE HEARD IT SAID—AND MY GUESS IS YOU HAVE TOO—
that beauty is in the eye of the beholder. But I've never been
certain it's true.

Think about it for a moment.

It sounds nice. I'll give you that. A way for every face to be
beautiful, if only you wait for the right pair of eyes. If only you
wait long enough. I'll even grant you that beauty isn't universal.
A girl who is considered drop-dead gorgeous in a town by the
sea may find herself completely overlooked in a village the next
county over.

Even so, *beauty is in the eye of the beholder* doesn't quite work,
does it?

Because there's something missing, and I can even tell you what: the belief we all harbor in our secret heart of hearts that beauty stands alone. That, by its very nature, it is obvious. In other words, Beauty with a capital *B*.

Beauty is in the eye of the beholder.

Now that's another statement entirely.

And what it means, as far as I can see, is that those of us whose looks aren't of the capital *B* variety can pretty much stop holding our breaths, stop waiting for the right eyes to show up and gaze upon us. Our Beauty—or, more precisely, our lack thereof—has already been established. It's as plain as the noses on our small *b* faces.

That sounds more like the way things actually work, doesn't it?

I suppose you could say that finding out just what a pair of eyes can do, and what they can't, is what the story I'm about to tell you is really all about. It will come as no surprise that it is, of course, my story. Which means I should probably back up and introduce myself.

Annabelle Evangeline Delaurier. That is my name. After my father's mother and my mother's mother, in that order. But, though it was my father who decided the entirety of what I would be called, it was my mother who sealed my fate and set my tale in motion. For she was the one who decreed I would be known as *Belle*, a name that means Beauty in the land of my birth.

There were problems with this decision, though nobody

realized it at the time. Two problems, to be precise: my older sisters, who displayed such extraordinary Beauty that they were famous for miles around.

My oldest sister was born at straight-up midnight, on a night so clear and cold it snatched the breath. A night that made the stars burn sharp and bright as knives. The baby's hair was as dark as the arc of heaven overhead, her eyes a blue both fierce and sparkling, like the stars.

In celebration of my sister's arrival, Maman, who has a tendency to be extravagant even in life's simple moments, named the infant Celestial Heavens, having earlier extracted a promise from my father that she could name their first child anything she wanted.

As I'm sure I don't need to point out, Celestial Heavens is quite a mouthful.

Fortunately for all concerned, and for my sister most of all, my father's more practical approach to life won out. Celestial Heavens the baby might be, but even before the ink on her birth certificate was dry, my sister was being called Celeste, as she has been from that day forward.

My second sister was born on the first day of the month of April, just as the sun rose over the horizon. Her hair was as golden as the sun's first light, her eyes as green as the meadow that the sun ran through on its way to make the morning. My father, now somewhat prepared for what might come next, took it in quiet stride when my mother named this daughter

April Dawn. By the time the baby had been tucked into her cradle that night, she was being called just April, and she has been ever since.

And then there was the day that I arrived.

At noon, on a day in September that could have been either spring or autumn, judging by the blueness of the sky. Or by the temperature, which was neither too hot nor too cold. A quiet, peaceful kind of day. The kind that, at its end, makes you wonder where the time has gone. A day that doesn't feel like a gift until it's done. For it's only as you're drifting off to sleep that you realize how happy you are, how happy you'd been every moment you were awake.

It was on just such a day as this that I was born.

Even my coming into the world was straightforward, for my mother later related that the time of her labor seemed neither too short, nor too long. Following these exertions, I was placed into my mother's arms. My father sat beside her on the bed, and both of them (or so I am told) gazed lovingly down at me. And if my father felt a small pang that his third child was yet another daughter and not a son, I'm willing to forgive him for it.

It wasn't that he valued daughters any less, but that, after two such extraordinary children, he was ready for one that was, perhaps, a little less remarkable. A child who might be more like him, follow in his footsteps rather than my mother's. And as he could not imagine how a girl's feet might accomplish such a task, in secret, my father had longed for a boy.

4

"Well, my dear?" my father asked my mother after several moments. He was referring, of course, to what I would be named, for, as always, the choice would be Maman's. She knew what to call my two sisters without hesitation. But here a curious and unexpected event transpired.

Accustomed as my mother was to the spectacular arrivals of Celeste and April, my appearance called forth not a single inspiration. Though her imagination was vivid, my mother simply could not conjure what to call a child who had arrived with so little fanfare, on a day that was so very unremarkable.

My mother opened her mouth, then closed it, without making a single sound. She took a breath, then tried again. And when this attempt also failed to produce a name, she tried a third time. Finally, she closed her mouth and kept it shut, looking at my father with beseeching eyes.

Fortunately, my father is quick on his feet, even when he isn't standing on them.

"My dear," he said to Maman once more. "You have given me a beautiful and healthy daughter, and surely that is gift enough. But I wonder if I might ask for one thing more. I wonder if you would allow *me* to name this child."

Her lips still firmly closed, my mother nodded her head, and my father bestowed a name he had long cherished: Annabelle, after his own mother, who had had the raising of him all on her own. Then, mindful of my mother's feelings, he gave me the name of her mother as well.

In this way, I became Annabelle Evangeline, and no sooner had my father proclaimed his choice than my mother recovered enough to announce that she wished me to be known as *Belle*. If I could not have an arrival quite as remarkable as those of my sisters, I could at least have an everyday name that, like my sisters, would match the Beauty I would surely become.

Allow me to set something straight at this point.

There's nothing actually wrong with the way I look. I have long brown hair that generally does what I ask it to, except on very rainy days when it does whatever it wants. I have eyes of a deep chestnut color that are not set too far from each other so that I appear to look over my own shoulder, nor so close that they appear to be trying to catch each other's glance across the bridge of my nose. And there's nothing wrong with my nose, either, thank you very much.

In fact, I have a face that is much like the day on which I was born. It contains neither too much of one thing, nor too little of another. A perfectly fine face. Just not an extraordinary face. And therein lies the problem. For the Beauty of my sisters can actually take a person's breath away.

I think my favorite example was when April surprised a would-be burglar in the middle of the night. She was no more than nine years old—which would have made me seven and Celeste eleven, just so you know where we are.

The thief, who turned out to be not much older than Celeste, had come to steal the brace of silver candlesticks that always stood on the sideboard in our dining room. April had gotten out of bed for a drink of water. They encountered each other in the downstairs hall.

All it took to subdue the boy was one look at April's golden hair, shining ever so faintly in the darkness, giving off a light of its own. The thief saw all that Beauty, sucked in an astonished breath, then fell to the floor like a sackful of rocks. The noise of this, not to mention April's sudden cry, roused the rest of the house. The would-be robber was still passed out cold, the candlesticks on the floor beside him, when my father summoned the constable.

The story has a happier ending than you might suppose. For April took pity on the lad and convinced my father to do the same.

Shortly after the constable arrived, and with his permission, Papa offered the unsuccessful thief, who had the extremely un-thief-like name of Dominic Boudreaux, a choice: Dominic could go to jail or he could go to sea. Papa is one of the most successful merchants in all our city. His ships sail to every part of the globe, and he had a ship scheduled to set sail with that morning's tide.

Not surprisingly, Dominic Boudreaux chose the second course. As a result, he departed for his new life almost as soon as he'd made up his mind to have one. To the astonishment of all concerned, Dominic took to the sea like a sailor born. He's been sailing for Papa ever since, for about ten years now.

Papa gave him command of the newest ship in the fleet when he turned twenty-one, the youngest man he'd ever raised to captain. When Papa asked Dominic what he thought his ship should be called, Dominic answered without hesitation: the *April Dawn*.

It's a nice story, isn't it? But I've told it to you for a reason other than the obvious one. Because what happened to Dominic and April in the middle of that night tells a second story. A tale about Beauty that I've often murmured to myself, but that I've never heard anyone else so much as whisper aloud. And that tale is this: Beauty does more than stand alone. It also creates a space around itself. Beauty casts its own shadow, because it finds its own way to shine.

There's a catch, of course: For every moment that Beauty shines bright, something—or someone—standing right beside it gets covered up by Beauty's shadow. Goes overlooked, unnoticed.

You can trust me on this one. I know what I'm talking about.

On the twenty-fifth day of September, ten days after my tenth birthday, it happened to me, for on that day I performed an act I never had before. I stepped between my two sisters, and the shadows cast by their two Beauties so overlapped each other that they completely filled the place in which I stood.

As a result, I disappeared entirely.

Two

I DIDN'T *LITERALLY* DISAPPEAR, OF COURSE. I WAS STILL right there, just like always. Or rather, not like always because, incredible as it may seem, I had never actually occupied the space between my sisters.

Maybe it was because Maman sensed the possibility of what did, in fact, occur. Or perhaps it was simply that, in spite of her sometimes impulsive nature, Maman liked everything, including her daughters, to be well-organized. Whatever the reason, until that fateful moment, I had never occupied the space between my sisters for the simple reason that we spent our lives in chronological order.

Celeste. April. Belle.

Everything about my sisters and me was arranged in this fashion, in fact. It was the way our beds were lined up in our bedroom; our places at the dining table, where we all sat in a row along one side. It was the order in which we got dressed each morning and had our hair brushed for one hundred and one strokes each night. The order in which we entered a room or left it, and were introduced to guests. The only exception was when we were allowed to open our presents all together, in a great frenzy of paper and ribbons, on Christmas morning.

This may seem very odd to you, and you may wonder why it didn't to any of us. All that I can say is that order in general, but most especially the order in which one was born, was considered very important in the place where I grew up. The oldest son inherited his father's house and lands. Younger daughters did not marry unless the oldest had first walked down the aisle. So if our household paid strict attention to which sister came first, second, and (at long last) third, the truth is that none of us thought anything about the arrangement at all.

Until the day Monsieur LeGrand came to call.

Monsieur LeGrand was my father's oldest and closest friend, though Papa had seen him only once and that when he was five years old. In his own youth, Monsieur LeGrand had been the boyhood friend of Papa's father, Grand-père Georges. It was Monsieur LeGrand who had brought to Grand-mère Annabelle the sad news that her young husband had been snatched off the deck of his ship by a wave that curled around him like a giant fist, then picked him up and carried him down to the bottom of the ocean.

In some other story, Monsieur LeGrand might have stuck around, consoled the young widow in her grief, then married her after a suitable period of time. But that story is not this one. Instead, soon after reporting his sad news, Monsieur LeGrand returned to the sea, determined to put as much water as he could between himself and his boyhood home.

Eventually, Monsieur LeGrand became a merchant specializing in silk, and settled in a land where silkworms flourished, a place so removed from where he'd started out that if you marked each city with a finger on a globe, you'd need both hands. Yet even from this great distance, Monsieur LeGrand did not forget his childhood friend's young son.

When Papa was old enough, Grand-mère Annabelle took him by the hand and marched him down to the waterfront offices of the LeGrand Shipping Company. For, though he no longer lived in the place where he'd grown up, Monsieur LeGrand maintained a presence in our seaport town. My father then began the process that took him from being the boy who swept the floors and filled the coal scuttles to the man who knew as much about the safe passage of sailors and cargo as anyone.

When that day arrived, Monsieur LeGrand made Papa his partner, and the sign above the waterfront office door was changed to read LEGRAND, DELAURIER AND COMPANY. But nothing

Papa ever did, not marrying Maman nor helping to bring three lovely daughers into the world, could entice Monsieur LeGrand back to where he'd started.

Over the years, he had become something of a legend in our house. The tales my sisters and I spun of his adventures were as good as any bedtime stories our nursemaids ever told. We pestered our father with endless questions to which he had no answers. All that he remembered was that Monsieur LeGrand had been straight and tall. This was not very satisfying, as I'm sure you can imagine, for any grown-up might have looked that way to a five-year-old.

Then one day—on my tenth birthday, to be precise—a letter arrived. A letter that caused my father to return home from the office in the middle of the day, a thing he never does. I was the first to spot Papa, for I had been careful to position myself near the biggest of our living room windows, the better to watch for any presents that might arrive.

At first, the sight of Papa alarmed me. His face was flushed, as if he'd run all the way from the waterfront. He burst through the door, calling for my mother, then dashed into the living room and caught me up in his arms. He twirled me in so great a circle that my legs flew out straight and nearly knocked Maman's favorite vase to the floor.

He'd had a letter, Papa explained when my feet were firmly on the ground. One that was better than any birthday present he could have planned. It came from far away, from the land where the silkworms flourished, and it informed us all that, at long last, Monsieur LeGrand was coming home.

Not surprisingly, this threw our household into an uproar. For it went without saying that ours would be the first house Monsieur LeGrand would come to visit. It also went without saying that everything needed to be perfect for his arrival.

The work began as soon as my birthday celebrations were complete. Maman hired a small army of extra servants, as those who usually cared for our house were not great enough in number. They swept the floors, then polished them until they gleamed like gems. They hauled the carpets out of doors and beat them. Every single picture in the house was taken down from its place on the walls and inspected for even the most minute particle of dust. While all this was going on, the walls themselves were given a new coat of whitewash.

But the house wasn't the only thing that got polished. The inhabitants got a new shine as well. Maman was all for us being reoutfitted from head to foot, but here, Papa put his foot down. We must not be extravagant, he said. It would give the wrong impression to Monsieur LeGrand. Instead, we must provide his mentor and our benefactor with a warm welcome that also showed good sense, by which my father meant a sense of proportion.

So, in the end, it was only Papa and Maman who had new outfits from head to foot. My sisters and I each received one new garment. Celeste, being the oldest, had a new dress. April had a new silk shawl. As for me, I was the proud owner of a new pair of shoes.

It was the shoes that started all the trouble, you could say. Or, to be more precise, the buckles.

They were made of silver, polished as bright as mirrors. They were gorgeous and I loved them. Unfortunately, the buckles caused the shoes to pinch my feet, which in turn made taking anything more than a few steps absolute torture. Maman had tried to warn me in the shoe shop that this would be the case, but I had refused to listen and insisted the shoes be purchased anyhow.

"She should never have let you have your own way in the first place," Celeste pronounced on the morning we expected Monsieur LeGrand.

My sisters and I were in our bedroom, watching and listening for the carriage that would herald Monsieur LeGrand's arrival. Celeste was standing beside her dressing table, unwilling to sit lest she wrinkle her new dress. April was kneeling on a cushion near the window, the silk shawl draped around her shoulders, her own skirts carefully spread out around her. I was the only one actually sitting down. Given the choice between the possibility of wrinkles or the guarantee of sore feet, I had decided to take my chances with the wrinkles.

But though I was seated, I was hardly sitting still. Instead, I turned my favorite birthday present and gift from Papa—a small knife for wood carving that was cunningly crafted so that the blade folded into the handle—over and over between my hands, as if the action might help to calm me.

Maman disapproves of my wood carving. She says it isn't ladylike and is dangerous. I have pointed out that I'm just as likely to stab myself with an embroidery needle as I am to cut myself with a wood knife. My mother remains unconvinced, but Papa is delighted that I inherited his talent for woodwork.

"And put that knife away," Celeste went on. "Do you mean to frighten Monsieur LeGrand?"

"Celeste," April said, without taking her eyes from the street scene below. "Not today. Stop it."

Thinking back on it now, I see that Celeste was feeling just as nervous and excited as I was. But Celeste almost never handles things the way I do, or April either, for that matter. She always goes at things head-on. I think it's because she's always first. It gives her a different view of the world, a different set of boundaries.

"Stop what?" Celeste asked now, opening her eyes innocently wide. "I'm just saying Maman hates Belle's knives, that's all. If she shows up with one today, Maman will have an absolute fit."

"I know better than to take my wood-carving knife into the parlor to meet a guest," I said as I set it down beside me on my dressing table.

"Well, yes, you may *know* better, but you don't always *think*, do you?" Celeste came right back. She swayed a little, making her new skirts whisper to the petticoats beneath as they moved from side to side. Celeste's new dress was a pale blue, almost an exact match for her eyes. She'd wanted it every bit as much as I'd wanted my new shoes.

"For instance, if you'd thought about how your feet might *feel* instead of how they'd *look*, you'd have saved yourself a lot of pain, and us the trouble of listening to you whine."

I opened my mouth to deny it, then changed my mind. Instead, I gave Celeste my very best smile. One that showed as many of my even, white teeth as I could. I have very nice teeth. Even Maman says so.

I gave the bed beside me a pat. "If you're so unconcerned about the way *you* look," I said sweetly, "why don't you come over here and sit down?"

Celeste's cheeks flushed. "Maybe I don't want to," she answered.

"And maybe you're a phony," I replied. "You care just as much about how you look as I do, Celeste. It just doesn't suit you to admit it, that's all."

"If you're calling me a liar—" Celeste began hotly.

"Be quiet!" April interrupted. "I think the carriage is arriving!"

Quick as lightning, Celeste darted to the window, her skirts billowing out behind her. I got to my feet, doing my best to ignore how much they hurt, and followed. Sure enough, in the street below, the grandest carriage I had ever seen was pulling up before our door.

"Oh, I can't see his face!" Celeste cried in frustration as we saw a gentleman alight. A moment later, the peal of the front doorbell echoed throughout the house. April got to her feet, smoothing out her skirts as she did so. In the pit of my stomach, I felt a group of butterflies suddenly take flight.

I really *did* care about the way I looked, if for no other reason than how I looked and behaved would reflect upon Papa and Maman. All of us wanted to make a good impression on Monsieur LeGrand.

"My dress isn't too wrinkled, is it?" I asked anxiously, and felt the butterflies settle down a little when it was Celeste who answered.

"You look just fine."

"The young ladies' presence is requested in the parlor," our housekeeper, Marie Louise, announced from the bedroom door. Marie Louise's back is always as straight as a ruler, and her skirts are impeccably starched. She cast a critical eye over the three of us, then gave a satisfied nod.

"What does Monsieur LeGrand look like, Marie Louise?" I asked. "Did you see him? Tell us!"

Marie Louise gave a sniff to show she disapproved of such questions, though her eyes were not unkind.

"Of course I saw him," she answered, "for who was it who answered the door? But I don't have time to stand around gossiping any more than you have time to stand around and listen. Get along with you, now. Your parents and Monsieur LeGrand are waiting for you in the parlor."

With a rustle of skirts, she left.

My sisters and I looked at one another for a moment, as if catching our collective breath.

"Come on," Celeste said. And, just like that, she was off. April followed hard on her heels.

"Celeste," I begged, my feet screaming in agony as I tried to keep up. "Don't go so fast. Slow down."

But I was talking to the open air, for my sisters were already gone. By the time I made it to the bedroom door, they were at the top of the stairs. And by the time I made it to the top of the stairs, they were at the bottom. Celeste streaked across the entryway, then paused before the parlor door, just long enough to give her curls a brisk shake and clasp her hands in front of her as was proper. Then, without a backward glance, she marched straight into the parlor with April trailing along behind her.

Slowly, I descended the stairs, then came to a miserable stop in the downstairs hall.

Should I go forward, I wondered, *or should I stay right where I am?*

No matter who got taken to task over our entry later—and someone most certainly would be—there could be no denying that I was the one who would look bad at present. I was the one who was late. I'd probably already embarrassed my parents and insulted our honored guest. *Perhaps I should simply slink away, back to my room,* I thought. I could claim I'd suddenly become ill between the top of the stairs and the bottom, that it was in everyone's best interest that I hadn't made an appearance, particularly Monsieur LeGrand's.

And perhaps I could flap my arms and fly to the moon.

That's when I heard the voices drifting out of the parlor.

There was Maman's, high and piping like a flute. Papa's with its quiet ebb and flow that always reminds me of the sea. Celeste and April I could not hear at all, of course. They were children and would not speak unless spoken to first. And then I heard a voice like the great rumble of distant thunder say:

"But where is *la petite Belle?*"

And, just as real thunder will sometimes inspire my feet to carry me from my own room into my parents', so too the sound of what could be no other than Monsieur LeGrand's voice carried me through the parlor door and into the room beyond. As if to make up for how slowly my feet had moved before, I overshot my usual place in line. Instead of ending up at the end of the row, next to April, I came to a halt between my two sisters. April was to my left and Celeste to my right. We were out of order for the first and only time in our lives.

I faltered, appalled. For I was more than simply out of place; I was also directly in front of Monsieur LeGrand.

Three

HE REALLY *WAS* TALL. SO TALL IT ALMOST MADE ME DIZZY
to tilt my neck back to look up at him. Unlike the implica-
tions of his name, Monsieur LeGrand wasn't relaxed and round.
Instead, he was all sharpness and angles—like one of the tools
Papa keeps in his workshop for shaping wood. His skin was
tanned, permanently stained by the combination of sun and salt.
Even his eyes reminded me of the sea, for they were the blue-
black of deep water.

I noticed all this in the time it took his eyes to scan the
room, as if I might be hiding in one of the corners.

"Where is *la petite Belle?*" he asked again. "Is she not coming?"

How is it possible he does not see me? I wondered. For I was standing right in front of him, so close that I could have taken no more than two steps and touched his toes with mine.

I pulled in a breath, determined to speak and call his attention to me, but felt the air refuse to leave my lungs. My entire body began to flush with embarrassment, the way it does when you've been caught in an outright lie—for suddenly it seemed that this was precisely what had happened. Monsieur LeGrand's inability to see me had exposed a falsehood. The only problem was that I didn't have the faintest idea what it was.

I've got to get back to my proper place, I thought. *Surely everything will start to make sense again if I can just get back to my place in line.*

Slowly, fearing to call attention to myself now, I took one step back, while my sisters each took a sidling step toward each other. The space between them was now filled. There was no room for me anymore. Safely behind their backs, I took two quick sidesteps to the left. I was on the far side of April now. All I had to do was take two more steps, forward this time, and I would be exactly where I was expected to be.

Releasing the breath I'd been holding, I eased forward into my proper place in line.

"Ah." I heard Maman exhale, as if she'd been holding her breath as well.

"Here she is, Alphonse," Papa said, for that was Monsieur LeGrand's name. "Here is Belle."

I stepped forward again, intending to make a curtsy, though

my legs had begun to tremble so much that I was afraid they might not hold me if I tried. But before I could even make the attempt, Monsieur LeGrand stepped forward as well. To my astonishment, he knelt down—in that way grown-ups have sometimes when meeting a young person for the first time. Not condescendingly, just wanting to view the world from their perspective.

For several moments, Monsieur LeGrand and I gazed at each other, face-to-face and eye-to-eye. I've often wondered whether I'd have seen what happened next if we hadn't been so close.

For, ever so slowly, Monsieur LeGrand's face began to change. The only way I can describe it is to say it became kind. As if he found the way to smooth out all the harsh angles until what lay beneath was revealed: kindness in its purest, most generous form.

I forgot my aching feet and trembling legs then, as a terrible possibility, an explanation for everything that had happened since I'd first entered the room, shot like a bolt of lightning across my ten-year-old mind.

What if my name was wrong? What if Monsieur LeGrand's kindness was not only a simple gift but also a consolation prize, one designed to make up for the fact that I was not a Beauty, not truly *Belle* at all? What if my name was not my true measure, but was the lie I told?

It would explain so much, I thought. Such as why Monsieur

LeGrand had not seen me standing between my sisters, as close as the reach of his arm. He had looked for a Beauty to go with theirs, but he had failed to find it. My face did not live up to the promise of my name.

My legs did give way then, and I heard Monsieur LeGrand give a startled exclamation as I suddenly swayed and closed my eyes. If I stared into his one moment longer, I feared I might begin to weep, for now I could see that there was more than kindness in his look. There was pity there as well.

"Why, Belle!" I heard my mother exclaim as, with a swish of silk, she, too, knelt down. I sensed Monsieur LeGrand getting to his feet even as I felt my mother's arms enfold me. I leaned my head against her shoulder, drinking in the scent of lavender that always hovers about her like a soft and fragrant cloud.

"Whatever is the matter? Are you ill?" my mother inquired.

Maman, my heart pounded out in hard, fast strokes. *Oh, Maman. Maman. Why didn't you say something? Why didn't you warn me that this day would come?*

For I had heard more than just the way my mother's dress moved. My legs might have been refusing to function, but my ears still worked just fine. Running through my mother's voice like a strand of errant-colored thread was a tone that was the perfect match for the expression in Monsieur LeGrand's eyes. Maman pitied me too.

It must be true, then, I thought.

I was not a Beauty, and my own mother knew it.

How long had she known? Surely she must have believed I was beautiful on the day of my birth, or she would not have insisted on calling me *Belle*.

When had I lost my Beauty? I wondered. Where had it gone?

"Belle?" I suddenly heard my father's quiet voice say. "Are you all right?"

At the sound of it, I felt the rapid beating of my heart begin to slow. For Papa's voice sounded just as it always did. There was nothing in it to show that he had noticed anything different about me, nothing to indicate that anything was wrong.

And suddenly, with that, nothing was. I opened my eyes and stepped out of the circle of my mother's arms.

"I'm fine, Papa," I assured him.

Maman got to her feet and went to stand at Papa's side, a faint frown between her brows. I curtsied then, the buckles on my new shoes squeezing like vise grips. As I straightened, I snuck a quick glance upward at Monsieur LeGrand. If his expression held any hidden meaning now, for the life of me, I could not see it.

"I am pleased to meet you, Monsieur," I went on. "I apologize for causing a fuss. . . . I didn't mean . . . it's just . . ."

"It's just that she's so excited to meet you, Alphonse," my father said, coming to my rescue. "It's all she's talked about since your letter arrived. It came on her birthday. Did I tell you that? She declared it her favorite gift."

"Is that so?" Monsieur LeGrand inquired, and then he smiled. His eyes grew brighter, and all the wrinkles in his face seemed to join together to form a new pattern of lines more complex than that on any sea chart. "That's the nicest bit of news I've had in a good long while."

"Yes, Marie Louise?" my mother's voice slid beneath Monsieur LeGrand's.

"Luncheon is served, Madame," Marie Louise murmured from just inside the parlor door. Three paces in and not a step farther unless she is requested to do so.

"Thank you," my mother said, nodding. I stepped back, so that my sisters and I were standing in a perfect straight line.

We all knew what would happen next. Monsieur LeGrand would offer Maman his arm. He would lead her into the dining room, pull out her chair, then sit down to her right, the position a guest of honor always occupies. Papa would take Celeste in. April and I would follow along behind. All of us would be in our proper place, our proper order. Things would be completely back to normal.

But Monsieur LeGrand surprised us all. For instead of turning to offer his arm to Maman, he closed the distance between us and offered it to me.

"Will you give me the pleasure of taking you in to lunch, *ma Belle*?" he asked as he executed an expert bow. "Think of it as the rest of your birthday present."

I laughed in astonished delight before I could help myself.

For here was a gift I had never even thought to wish for: the chance to be first in line.

I shot a quick glance in Papa's direction and saw his lips lift in an encouraging smile. I didn't quite dare to glance at Celeste, who was now destined to follow along behind. I wondered if she would recognize my back, for it would be unfamiliar to her. I remembered to keep it perfectly straight as I dipped a curtsy in response to Monsieur LeGrand's bow.

"Thank you, Monsieur," I said. "I accept your gift with pleasure."

Both of us straightened up, and I stepped forward to meet him. Slipping my fingers into the crook of his elbow, I let him lead me out of the parlor and into the hall.

It wasn't until at least an hour later, when lunch was nearly over, that I realized I'd walked the entire distance from the parlor to the dining room without feeling the pinch of my new shoes at all.

Four

LATE THAT NIGHT I LAY IN BED, ROLLING THE EVENTS OF the day over in my mind.

The rest of Monsieur LeGrand's visit had passed as smoothly as the silk he had exported for so long. In the excitement of the day and listening to his stories of lands far away, I had allowed the strange and unhappy moments in the parlor to steal away to the farthest corner of my mind.

This was not the same as saying I'd banished them forever, though. They were still there, simply biding their time. Now that the house was quiet and my mind had no other distractions, the memories of what had happened crept forward once more.

Belle. I mouthed the word silently in the darkness. *I am Annabelle Evangeline Delaurier, but everybody calls me Belle.*

Everybody called me Beauty, in other words. But what if what I had feared in the parlor this afternoon was true, and I wasn't so very Beautiful after all?

How do you recognize Beauty when you see it?

What *is* Beauty, anyhow?

I turned my head, the better to see April's where she rested in the bed beside mine. Even in the dim light of the moon coming through the window, April's hair glimmered ever so faintly, like a spill of golden coins. I was pretty sure there wasn't another head in our entire city that could even dream of doing this, of shining in the dark.

If anything is Beautiful, surely that is it, I thought.

But was shining hair enough? Was that all it took to make my sister Beautiful? Or was it not also the way her green eyes sparkled when she laughed? The way her laughter sounded like clear water dancing over stones. Everything about April was like a hand outstretched, inviting you to reach out to join her.

That is truly what makes her Beautiful, I thought.

I lifted myself up onto one elbow now, straining to see beyond April to Celeste's sleeping form. My oldest sister did not give off her own light. If anything, it was just the opposite. The place where she lay seemed plunged in shadow, as if Celeste always carried some part of midnight, the time of her birth, with her.

Whereas April's looks shone out to meet you, Celeste's looks were of a different kind. Something about her always seemed mysterious, hidden from view, even when she was standing in direct sunlight. She made you look once, then look again, as if to make certain you hadn't missed anything the first time around.

That is Beauty too, I decided. Not as comfortable a kind of Beauty as April's, perhaps, but Beauty just the same, for it made you want more. So that made both my sisters Beautiful with a capital *B*.

Where does that leave me? I wondered.

Yes, I know. It sounds as if I was edging right up to self-pity, but I swear to you that wasn't how it seemed at the time. It was simply the logical next question, the next piece of the puzzle I had suddenly discovered I needed to solve.

All of us come to some moment in our childhoods when we realize that the world is bigger than what we have previously known. Larger than we imagined it could be. Wider than the reach of our arms, even when they are stretched out as far as they can go. That is what happened to me on the day of Monsieur LeGrand's visit, I think. As if standing between my two sisters had hidden me from view, but opened up the world all at the same time.

Before Monsieur LeGrand's arrival, I had never really taken the time to consider my relationship with my sisters. Or if I had, it was only to think about our order: Celeste. April. Belle.

But if my name was not the true match to my face, was last

my true place in line? What if there was something different mapped out for me? If I didn't even know myself, how could I begin to find out what that something was?

All of a sudden, I couldn't bear lying in bed one moment longer. My body felt foreign, as if it belonged to someone else. So I tossed back the covers and swung my legs over the side of the bed and sat up, hissing ever so slightly as my bare feet hit the cold floor. Quietly, so as not to awaken my sleeping sisters in all their loveliness, I pulled a robe on over my nightdress, slid my feet into my oldest and most soft-soled pair of shoes, and slipped out the bedroom door.

A house is a strange thing at night, even when that house is your own. For even the most comfortable, well-lived-in of houses has its secrets. If you get up unexpectedly in the night, you can sometimes catch a glimpse of them. Our house seemed to whisper to itself in voices that were quickly hushed as I hurried along its darkened corridors.

Was it talking about me? Discussing my lost Beauty, perhaps? I pursed my lips, pressing them tightly together so I wouldn't be tempted to pose the question. I wasn't all that sure I wanted to know.

I sped along the upstairs hallway on swift and silent feet, then hurried down the stairs at a pace I would dearly have loved earlier that day. I swung right, toward the kitchen at the back of the house. Easing open the door, I poked my head around it, then slid all the way inside.

There, resting on the kitchen windowsill, between a pot of marjoram on one side and oregano on the other, was a single lantern, its flame burning clear and bright. At the sight of this, I felt some of the terrible strangeness that pulled me out of bed begin to ease.

Papa was working late in his workshop.

Do you feel closer to one of your parents than to the other? I do, and I here admit that, much as I love my mother, I have always been closer to Papa. I think it's that the way his mind works makes sense to me, in a way that Maman's never does. I understand the world better when I catch a glimpse of it through Papa's eyes. Even when he shows me a bigger piece of it than what I'm used to, it's still a world I recognize.

And so it was to Papa that I had always gone with any new discovery, any important question, any joy or hurt or sorrow. Most of these conferences had taken place where my father did his own problem-solving: his workshop. Papa had built it with his own two hands, right in our backyard. The lighted lantern was the signal that he was there.

I pulled my robe a little tighter to my chest, for the autumn night was clear and I knew it would be cold. I eased open the kitchen door as quietly as I could, and slipped outside. A path made of broken seashells stretched before me, gleaming pale in the moonlight. Papa had created this, too, so that it would be easy to see the way to and from the house. I loved the faint crunching the shells made underfoot, which also helped to warn Papa of anyone's approach. He used sharp tools inside the workshop. Surprise was not always welcome.

Reaching the door, I used the secret knock I'd developed when I was three, thinking it was the height of cleverness: two knocks, a pause, and then two more. My father's voice sounded even before I had finished knocking.

"Yes. Come in," he called.

I lifted the latch and pushed open the door, blinking a little at the sudden change of light. Papa kept the workshop very bright.

"Hello, Papa," I said.

"Well," my father said, as if clearing his head of whatever thoughts had been there before I arrived and making room for whatever I might have brought with me. "Hello, Belle. Come all the way in and shut the door, will you? You'll let in the moths, otherwise."

I did as I was asked, leaving a small cloud of moths jockeying for position outside the window, trying to reach the lights inside. I always feel sorry for them. They seem so frantic. Not only that, they always come in last, just like I do. Most people prefer butterflies.

"You're up late," my father commented. He set down the project on which he had been working, and I recognized it as a jewelry box. Monsieur LeGrand had given Maman a fine string of pearls just that afternoon. No doubt Papa was making her a special place to store them.

"I was just about to take a break and make some hot chocolate," he said. "Might I interest you in some?"

"Can I have cinnamon in mine?" I asked at once. This was the way I liked it best. It was Papa's favorite too.

"I think that can be arranged," he answered with a smile. I took the spot he'd vacated as he went to the small potbellied stove in the corner of the room, stirred up the coals, and put a pan of milk on to warm.

I watched Papa work, cutting slices of chocolate so thin they curled like wood shavings, before plopping them into the steaming pot with each deft flick of the knife. Papa makes hot chocolate the same way he makes everything else, with smooth, deliberate, and precise movement. I love these qualities about him. He's self-assured, like he's thought things through and knows where he's going. It makes me feel that it's safe to follow him, even into unknown territory.

When the hot chocolate was prepared to his satisfaction, Papa poured two mugs full, slid a stick of cinnamon into each, then brought me mine. Papa sat down beside me and we sipped in thoughtful silence for several moments. I also love this about my father. He doesn't badger me to get going right away. He always lets me take my time.

I was halfway through my mug and Papa had almost finished his before the time was right.

"Papa, may I ask you something?"

"You may ask me anything you like, *ma Belle*," my father

replied. He set his mug down, as if to indicate he was ready for whatever I might ask him. As for myself, I took one more fortifying sip.

"Am I Beautiful?" I blurted out.

It wasn't precisely the question I'd intended to start with, but sometimes, even when you tell yourself you want to ease into things, the question you want to ask the most just pops right out of your mouth.

My father's eyebrows leaped toward his hairline. This was the only sign that my question had taken him by surprise.

"Of course you are beautiful, Belle," he said.

But I could tell that he hadn't really understood what I meant. The way my father said the word, it was just another adjective and nothing more. I stirred my chocolate with my cinnamon stick, trying to figure out how to ask in a way that would tell him what I needed to know.

"But am I *Beautiful*?" I said again, trying to give the word the extra emphasis I thought it deserved. "As Beautiful as Celeste and April?"

My father picked up his mug, a frown between his brows. "What makes you ask that?"

"Papa," I said, drawing out the second syllable, and trying not to let the fear that he was putting me off get the better of me. "Why does anyone ask a question? Because I want to know the answer."

"Now, Belle," my father began.

"I know," I interrupted. "Pretend we're bolts of silk you're thinking about buying. We're all lined up together, but you can choose only one. Which one of us would you want the most?"

"But surely that question is impossible to answer," my father replied. "For it would depend on why I wanted it. Everything is beautiful in its own way, *ma Belle*, even if you have to look hard to find it."

I felt a hard knot form in the pit of my stomach. "I'm not sure that can be right, Papa. How can it be real Beauty if you have to look hard to see it? Isn't Beauty supposed to be easy to recognize?"

My father narrowed his eyes. "To tell you the truth, I don't think I've ever thought of it in quite that way before," he said, drawing the words out slowly. "I think I'd like a few more minutes to think it over, if that's all right."

This is the downside to the fact that my father never rushes others. You can't rush him, either.

"That's fine, Papa," I said grudgingly.

Giving my father more time was one thing. Sitting still while he pondered my fate was quite another. So, while my father cogitated, I got up from the bench and prowled around the workshop. I knew its nooks and crannies well, and not simply because I often came to talk with my father. I have what Papa calls *quick hands*, the hands of a true wood-carver. If I hold a piece of wood long enough, I can hear the story that it has to tell.

Actually, that's not quite the right way to put it. What really happens is that I *feel* the story the wood is telling. It's as if I become part of the tree the wood once belonged to. It begins with a tingling in my hands, then it flows up my arms and throughout my body. When the story reaches my heart, I can see the image that the wood has cherished deep inside itself. After that, it is simply a matter of gently carving away the extra wood.

We discovered my talent quite by accident when I was about six. Playing outside one day, I picked up a small branch that had come down in a windstorm. Instead of discarding it, I insisted on taking it straight to Papa's workshop. It took a while for him to understand that I was both sincere and determined when I claimed there was a bird inside and I wished to carve it out of the branch. Maman, I think, was genuinely alarmed.

But eventually Papa took me at my word, sitting beside me on the workbench, adding the strength and skill of his hands when my own weren't quite enough. By the end of the day, a small carved bird perched at one end of the branch. All that was needed was a dash of red paint, my father said, to complete the image of a cardinal. I've been a wood-carver ever since.

Now I selected a piece at random—alder, I think—and fetched my carving tools from the workbench Papa had made for me. Then I dragged a packing crate over so that it faced the bench on which my father sat. The piece of alder wasn't large, only a little longer than the palm of my hand, and newly cut, for all its edges felt hard and clean to the touch. I held it in my hands on my lap for a moment, feeling the tingling first in my hands and then my wrists before it shot straight up my arms.

All right, then, I thought. *I see you well enough.* I opened the leather satchel, drew out the knife I wanted, and began to carve.

Five

AFTER WHAT FELT LIKE A GREAT DEAL OF TIME HAD GONE by, my father finally spoke. "I am not sure what to make of what you've asked me, Belle."

I concentrated on my carving, not letting my eyes stray to Papa's face.

"I never thought to compare you and your sisters, one to the other," my father went on. "Even when you stand all together, I see you one by one."

I pulled in a breath to protest that this could not be the case, then expelled it slowly. For I could tell my father was speaking the truth. Goods he compares on a daily basis because he must. But I realized I had never heard him compare one person to another. If anything, he compares you to yourself. Where you are now versus where he thinks you might be able to go. This is the ability that enabled him to give Dominic Boudreaux a second chance. As if Papa could literally see there was more to Dom than met most eyes.

"And as for beauty being something you must see at first glance, I don't think that can be right either," my father went on.

I gouged into the wood and flicked a piece away. "I think you're wrong, Papa."

"I don't see why," my father said, not arguing, but in a tone that told me he didn't think I was making any sense at all. "Don't they say that beauty is in the eye of the beholder?"

The knife jerked, skittering down the side of the alder to bite deep into the pad of my left hand. I didn't even feel the pain. Instead, I watched the blood well up, then run down onto my white nightgown.

In a quiet voice I asked, "But what if people can't see you at all? What if you're as good as invisible, Papa?"

"For heaven's sake, Belle!" my father exclaimed. He got up quickly, crossed to where I sat, and knelt in front of me. Papa carefully eased the wood and knife from my fingers and set them on the floor beside him. He pulled a clean handkerchief from the pocket of his smock and placed it against my cut, curling my right hand over my left to apply pressure to make the bleeding stop.

"I think it's high time you told me what the matter really

is," my father said. "In all these years, I've never known you to cut yourself."

"He didn't see me," I choked, and felt the words burn all the way up my throat. "He didn't see me, but I was standing right in front of him."

My father sat back on his heels. "Who didn't see you?" he demanded. "What are you talking about?"

"This afternoon," I said, answering the questions in reverse order. "Monsieur LeGrand."

My blood was seeping through the handkerchief now, in spite of my best efforts. The cut was deep, perhaps deep enough to leave a scar.

"This afternoon," my father said. "In the parlor, do you mean?"

I nodded. "I didn't mean to be late." My words came out in a great rush. "But my feet hurt and Celeste was going so fast and she wouldn't stop. So when I finally came in, I went too far. I ended up between Celeste and April, right in front of Monsieur LeGrand.

"But he didn't see me, Papa. He *couldn't* see me, and I think . . ." I paused, pulled in a shaky breath. "I think that I know why."

"And what is it that you think you know?" my father asked.

I began to cry then, hot, fat tears that slipped down my cheeks and fell onto the handkerchief, turning my red blood the pink of my mother's favorite rose.

"I think it's because my name is wrong. It doesn't match my face. I shouldn't be called Belle, because I'm not Beautiful. Not really. Not like Celeste and April are. That's why Monsieur LeGrand couldn't see me. He looked for a face to go with theirs, a Beautiful face. Only I don't have one. You can ask Maman if you don't believe me. She knows it's true. I saw it in her eyes."

My father looked as though I'd taken the piece of wood I'd been carving and knocked him over the head with it.

"Why, Belle," he murmured. "Belle."

"But that's just the problem, don't you understand?" I cried out. "I'm not *Beautiful*. My name is nothing but a lie. I don't want to be *Belle* anymore, Papa."

"Then who do you want to be?" my father asked quietly.

"I don't know," I sobbed. For this was the crux of the problem. "I don't know."

At this, my father stood and plucked me from the packing crate. Then he sat down upon it himself, settling me into his lap the way he'd done when I was very small. I tucked my head into the notch of his neck and cried as though I might never stop. My father remained silent throughout.

His arms around me were gentle, and even through my shaking, I could feel the beat of his heart against mine, firm and sure and strong. At last, my tears subsided and I let my head rest against his shoulder, pulling in long, deep breaths. Still, my father held his tongue.

"Couldn't I be Annabelle?" I asked. "I think, maybe . . ."

My voice wobbled and I took a breath to steady it. "Maybe if people weren't expecting to see a Beauty in the first place, it might be easier when it turns out I'm not."

My father was silent for several moments more, just long enough that I had to resist squirming within the circle of his arms.

"Annabelle is a fine name," he said at last. "It was my mother's name and I chose it for you myself. But I'm not so sure that changing what you're called will accomplish what you want it to, my little one.

"We all are more than what others call us, whether we like our names or not. We are also who we choose to be and what we decide to make of ourselves. Changing your name won't change that, nor will it change who you are inside."

"Oh, Papa," I sighed. Just this once, I would have liked it if he'd let me have my way. "Don't you ever answer just *yes* or *no*?"

"Sometimes," my father said. And I heard myself laugh before I quite realized what I'd done.

"There now, that's better," Papa declared, and he dropped a kiss on the top of my head. "I am sorry that what happened today has given you such pain, *ma petite Belle*. But you must remember that you are still young. Perhaps you and your name just need a little more time to find each other."

"Papa," I said, keeping my voice as neutral as I could. "Are you by any chance telling me I need to grow up?"

This time it was my father who laughed. He set me on my feet, then rose and gave a mighty stretch.

"I don't think I would have put it *quite* that way, but I suppose I do mean that." Then he knelt in front of me once again, reaching out to gently take me by the shoulders.

"I'm not quite sure what happened today," my father went on. "First impressions can be tricky things, for they can be both shallow and lasting, all at once. But of one thing I am absolutely certain: Anyone with the right eyes and heart to match will see your beauty, Belle. If not at first, then for the long run. Whether or not your beauty is like your sisters' is another thing entirely. Personally, I think that's beside the point."

"It doesn't feel beside the point," I said.

My father kissed my forehead. "I know it doesn't."

"Don't tell me," I said, sighing. "I'm going to have to wait to grow up for this one too."

"I'm afraid so," Papa said with a smile. "Now, how's the hand?"

"Better." I held it out. Papa eased the bloodstained handkerchief away from my skin. The place where the knife had slipped had left an angry red gash, but the bleeding had stopped.

"That's good," my father said. "We'll wash it when we get back to the kitchen, then bandage it up."

"We're going to have to tell Maman, aren't we?" If it had been a little cut, I might have gotten away without Maman noticing, but a bandage was going to be hard to disguise.

My father nodded sympathetically. "I'm afraid so. But I will make sure she knows that you were being careful. If she asks, I'll say I posed a question that took you by surprise. Not that we need go into the subject matter, of course," he added.

"Thank you, Papa," I said.

"*Ça ne fait rien,*" my father said. "It's nothing, little one." He fell silent, as if trying to decide whether to say more. "Though you know," he finally said, "perhaps if you spoke with your mother—"

"No," I said at once, for I could see where he was going. As far as I was concerned, there was no need to share my feelings regarding the unfortunate combination of my name and face with Maman. I had learned what she believed that afternoon. There was no point in having a discussion.

"If you say so," said my father. "Now, show me what you were carving, and then we will go in."

I bent to retrieve the wood, and held it out. Papa and I regarded it together. He grunted in surprise.

"That's Alphonse," he said. And so it was.

My father took it from me and held it up, the better to see it in the workshop light.

"That is a very clever likeness, Belle," he pronounced. "Not complete—you hardly had time enough for that. But I think that you have captured him, even so." He chuckled and ran his thumb along the wood. "You see how that bump in the wood is precisely like the bump on his nose?"

"I'm glad you like it, Papa," I said.

My father's expression grew thoughtful. "I think you have

a Gift, Belle," he said softly, and here, at last, I heard the capital letter in his voice. "I would like it if you could believe that true beauty springs from the same place."

"And where is that?" I asked.

"Why, from the heart, of course."

Again, I felt tears threaten. "I'd like that too," I said. "I'm just not sure I know how to believe it."

"Of course you don't," my father said simply. "That's what growing up is for."

"Oh, *Papa*," I said, my tone as good as rolling my eyes.

"I wouldn't worry about it too much," my father said, a twinkle in his eye. "In my experience, growing up happens on its own. But now I think I should get you to bed, before your mother comes looking for us and expresses a desire for both our hides."

"I love you, Papa," I said.

He reached down and took my uninjured hand in his. "And I love you, *ma petite Belle*. That sounds like a good starting place for whatever comes next, don't you think?"

"I do," I said.

Hand in hand, we walked in silence back to the house.

Six

WHAT HAPPENED NEXT WAS PRETTY MUCH JUST AS PAPA had predicted: I grew up, with my sisters beside me. But whereas Celeste and April journeyed along the paths I imagine all parents hope for their children—walkways with surfaces just bumpy enough to keep you paying attention and with enough curves so that you learn to think on your feet and develop character—the path I walked turned out to be a good deal more challenging.

I had promised my father I would try to be patient, try to give my name and face time to find each other. I fully intended to keep that promise, if for no other reason than I wanted Papa to be proud of me. There is a problem with unhappy memories, though; I wonder if you have discovered it.

Unhappy memories are persistent. They're specific, and it's the details that refuse to leave us alone. Though a happy memory may stay with you just as long as one that makes you miserable, what you remember softens over time. What you recall is simply that you were happy, not necessarily the individual moments that brought about your joy.

But the memory of something painful does just the opposite. It retains its original shape, all bony fingers and pointy elbows. Every time it returns, you get a quick poke in the eye or jab in the stomach. The memory of being unhappy has the power to hurt us long after the fact. We feel the injury anew each and every time we think of it. And so, despite my efforts to the contrary, this is how it was with me and the memory of my first meeting with Monsieur LeGrand.

It didn't matter that afterward he took notice of me no matter where I stood. That he moved in next door, we saw him every day, and I soon grew to love him and call him Grand-père Alphonse. The memory of our first meeting refused to leave me. Each time it surfaced, it created a new wound, brought me fresh pain. Pain and patience do not make for a comfortable combination.

And then, of course, there was Maman.

I'd like to say what happened that first afternoon with Grand-père Alphonse, the pity I had heard in my mother's voice even as she held me in her arms, came to make no difference in our relationship. But that would be a lie.

The truth is that it did make a difference. And not a little one at that. For every time my mother spoke my name, every time she looked at me, I felt her pity all over again.

For the first time in my life, I was glad to come last in line.

It meant I could lag behind, putting some distance between me and my Beautiful sisters—particularly when we had company or went out in public. Though we might arrive at some social engagement all together, I became adept at hanging back. The more distance I put between my sisters and me, the less painful the comparisons between us seemed to be. Eventually what people remembered most about me was that they didn't really remember me at all.

Celeste and April could always be found at the center of gatherings. Their faces were easy to call to mind. But the youngest Delaurier girl, the one named Belle, her image was much harder to summon, in spite of all her name might promise.

Finally, I just stayed home.

I expected Maman to protest, but she did not. If I'd needed any more proof that my mother thought I was not as Beautiful as her older daughters, she provided it then. For if she'd truly believed I was as Beautiful as my name proclaimed, she would have insisted I take my place in society with my sisters. But she did not. I was simply Annabelle Evangeline, not Celestial Heavens or April Dawn.

And so, while my sisters went to parties and balls, and did all the things girls do as they grow into young women, I did something entirely different: I spent my days in Papa's workshop. There, I carved every available piece of wood. The beauty I found within the wood always seemed much lovelier than my own countenance. In this way, the years went by. And if I was not completely happy, I wasn't exactly miserable either. It seemed a satisfactory compromise.

But even the best of compromises unravels sooner or later, and so it proved with mine. For I'd failed to consider the very thing that growing up means: passage of time. No matter where I spent my days, no matter what my face might look like, I was now a young lady. And young ladies have responsibilities to their families that cannot be shirked or avoided.

Or so my mother informed me at the breakfast table one fine morning in late summer when I was fifteen years old. It was just Maman, Celeste, April, and me. Papa had already departed for his waterfront office, which I considered significant when Maman chose that morning to announce that I would be required to attend the de la Montaignes' upcoming garden party.

The de la Montaignes were my father's bankers and one of the wealthiest families in the city. Their son, Paul, was considered the most eligible bachelor in town. Celeste had been discreetly mooning over him for months, ever since the invitation to the party had arrived. The de la Montaignes' garden party was an annual event, a highlight of the summer.

"I didn't have to go last year," I protested. "How come I have to go now?"

"Because you're almost sixteen," my mother answered, daintily spreading marmalade on a piece of toast. The look of great determination on her face, however, did not bode well for my changing her mind. When Maman spreads marmalade like that, there's pretty much no talking her out of anything.

"Almost old enough to be married," my mother went on. "Your sisters are certainly old enough to be."

So that's it, I thought. She was hoping for a match between Celeste and Paul de la Montaigne.

"He may be good-looking, but he's got no more sense than a pailful of earthworms," I remarked.

My mother paused, her eyes narrowing as she gazed in my direction, the knife with which she'd been applying the marmalade poised in midair. "Who?" she inquired.

"Paul de la Montaigne," I answered. "I heard Papa say so."

"You did not," Celeste said at once.

"I did so," I replied. "Though I wasn't meant to hear it," I relented, as I saw Celeste's face flush. "He was talking to Grand-père Alphonse. We were in the workshop. I was working in the corner and I think they forgot I was there."

"He should not have spoken so," Maman pronounced. She set the knife down on her plate with a sharp *click.* "But it makes no difference, as he did so in private. Paul de la Montaigne is the most suitable young man in our circle. Everybody knows it. And as Celeste is certainly one of the loveliest young women . . ."

Her voice trailed off, as there was little more to be said on the subject. She bit into her toast.

"So what do you want me along for?" I asked, when I was certain my mother's mouth was full. "Contrast?"

"Belle!" April said in a shocked voice.

My mother brought the palm of her free hand down on the tabletop so hard it made the silverware rattle. I watched her jaw work as she struggled to finish her food, the muscles of her throat constricting as she swallowed.

"No, I do not want you along for *contrast*," she said when she could speak, her voice hot enough to scald. As if in answer, I felt a painful blush rise in my face. I knew I'd gone too far.

"I want you along because you are a member of this family. Because you have family obligations, and it's time you began to honor them. You have been selfish long enough, Belle."

"Selfish!" I cried.

My mother placed her half-eaten toast precisely in the center of her plate, then rose to her feet.

"I will not discuss this matter with you any further," she said, her voice now cold as ice. "And you will not take it up with your father. I have spoken to him, and he agrees. It's time you take your place in society. You will wear the dress I select for you and attend the de la Montaignes' garden party in one week's time. Both your father and I expect you to behave in a way that does our family honor in public. It's unfortunate you can't seem to bring yourself to do so at home."

My mother flung her napkin onto her plate, and it landed squarely atop the piece of toast on which she'd so determinedly spread marmalade just moments before.

"You have ruined my appetite with your behavior," she said. "I am going upstairs to lie down. Be so good as to ring for Marie Louise and ask her to bring a cool compress for my forehead."

"I'll do it, Maman," Celeste said.

"Mais non!" my mother replied. "It must be Belle. It is time she acknowledged she is a part of this family. Celeste, you may see me to my room." She extended an arm. Celeste took it. Without a backward glance, my mother and my oldest sister walked out.

Slowly, as if my joints ached, I walked across the room to the bell cord. I gave it a swift tug to summon Marie Louise, and gave her my mother's instructions when she arrived. April sat quietly, her breakfast untouched.

"I suppose you think I'm selfish too," I said, when our housekeeper was gone.

"Not exactly," April answered. Her green eyes regarded me thoughtfully, though not without compassion. It was as if she was weighing how much more to say, how much more I could take.

"But I do think Maman has a point, Belle. The way things are now—it's just not right. I would think you'd feel that more than anyone. Don't you want to find someone who will see you for who you really are?"

"There's not very much chance of that," I said, unable to keep the bitterness from my voice. "Not with you and Celeste around."

April winced, and I instantly wished I could call the words back. It wasn't her fault she was so much more Beautiful than I was.

"I think," she said calmly and succinctly, without a hint of upset in her voice, "that you are wrong. And I think outsiders are not the only ones who fail to see you clearly."

"What's that supposed to mean?" I said.

April stood up. "Now who's being as dumb as a pailful of earthworms?" she asked. She walked to the door. "I saw the dress Maman picked out for you," she added. "It's every bit as lovely as mine or Celeste's."

And with that, she left me alone to my thoughts.

Seven

THE DAY OF THE GARDEN PARTY ARRIVED CLEAR AND bright. *Naturally,* I thought, somewhat sourly, as I stood in the bedroom, gazing at myself in all my new finery, trying to convince my stomach to calm down. It seemed that even the weather wished to impress the de la Montaignes.

I, of course, had prayed for rain all week long.

The episode at the breakfast table had not been mentioned again. Not even Papa brought it up, though I felt sure Maman had told him of it. By tacit agreement, neither my sisters nor I mentioned Paul de la Montaigne. Instead, we pretended it was a week like any other, and not one ending with an event of the utmost importance.

I caught a glimpse of movement in the mirror and realized I was passing my folding knife from hand to hand in an effort to calm myself. Deliberately, I set it on my nightstand and instead picked up the nosegay of flowers I was supposed to carry. Then I gazed back at my reflection.

April had been right, I had to admit. The dress Maman had chosen for me was lovely—every bit as lovely as those she'd chosen for Celeste, for April, and for herself. It was a pale color just edging into pink, like a spring rosebud caught in a late frost. The bodice was stitched with row upon row of tiny seed pearls and the full skirt seemed to go on for miles. I even had matching satin slippers, tied with pink ribbons. There would be no buckles to pinch my feet this time. Thin ropes of seed pearls were threaded through my hair, which fell in great rippling waves to my waist. A circlet of tiny pink rosebuds framed my forehead.

If I hadn't known for certain it was me, I never would have recognized myself.

I stared at the girl in the mirror, her long hair shining like mahogany in the afternoon sun. Eyes as dark as chestnut gazed right back.

Who are you? I wondered. *Are you Belle? Are you Beauty enough to stand beside your sisters without being afraid? To stand beside them proudly, sure of who you are both inside and out?*

I had absolutely no idea, but I knew this much: The time had come to find out.

* * *

The de la Montaignes' house was set upon a hill, its gardens cascading down the hillside in a series of graceful terraces, all of which overlooked the ocean. As much as I did not want to be impressed, even I had to admit I had never seen anything like it. Tables covered in white linens all but groaned under the weight of food and flowers. Women and girls in their finery looked like more beautiful blossoms.

My nerve held through our arrival, as Monsieur and Madame de la Montaigne received their guests, one by one.

"So this is the famous Belle," Henri de la Montaigne said as he took my hand and bowed low over it.

I had expected the richest man in town to be tall and imposing, sort of like Grand-père Alphonse. But my father's banker was round and pale. He looked like he rarely set foot out of doors. His hands were soft, making me self-conscious of the calluses on mine. I felt my courage teeter, then slowly slide down the hillside toward the sea.

What did he mean, "the famous Belle"?

"You must make sure my son catches a glimpse of you," Monsieur de la Montaigne went on.

"Of course, Monsieur, if that is what you wish," I said, remembering my manners, though I had no intention of doing any such thing. It was Celeste that Paul de la Montaigne ought to look at, not me.

"Excellent, excellent," Henri de la Montaigne proclaimed.

And then, much to my relief, he released my hand and turned his attention to the next guest in line.

My mother kept a sharp eye on me as we began to circulate, but soon she was engaged in conversation. The terrace became filled with so many people, it was easy to render myself invisible and fade into the crowd. You can call me a coward if you want to. I came close to doing so myself.

But the simple truth was that, once I didn't have to worry about the inevitable comparison when standing beside my sisters, I actually began to enjoy myself. The garden was gorgeous: lush green lawns and flowers overflowing carefully tended beds, all set against the jewel of the sea below. Slowly, I made my way from one garden terrace to the next, admiring the views, sampling various delicacies, until, at last, I came to the lowest level, the one by the water.

The garden here was all roses. *How Maman would love this,* I thought. She loved flowers of all sorts, but roses most of all. Her own rose garden was her pride and joy, the only place in our entire house and grounds she cared for all herself. Across the front of the terrace, as if framing images of the sea, stood a series of arbors with roses clambering joyfully up the sides and over the top. Each had a bench on either side. I headed for the one on the far right, certain it would be the most private.

It wasn't until I'd almost reached the bench that I realized it was occupied. Celeste was sitting there, a young man at her side. Though it had been many years since I had seen Paul de la Montaigne, I was certain it could be no other. He had his father's shape. I could not see his face, as his back was toward me, but I was sure that I would find it pale and round.

How on earth can Celeste even contemplate marrying him? I wondered as I stopped short. *Even if he is the most eligible bachelor in town.* I had no wish to disturb them, and I was certain an interruption was the last thing Celeste wanted. Fortunately, they had not seen me. They were too wrapped up in each other.

"I'm so pleased to get you alone," Paul de la Montaigne said, leaning toward Celeste. I eased myself backward, holding my breath. "There's a question I've been dying to ask you ever since you arrived."

I stopped in spite of myself. *He's really going to do it,* I thought. *Paul is going to ask Celeste to marry him.* I was going to have a brother-in-law who was as dumb as a pailful of earthworms.

"Yes, Paul?" Celeste asked expectantly.

"Is it true what they say about your sister?"

I froze in place, my eyes fixed on Celeste's face. Never had she looked more Beautiful, and never had I had more cause to admire her, for she never flinched. Not so much as a flicker of an eyelash revealed that Paul's question was not the one for which she'd hoped.

"I have two sisters. Which one?"

Paul de la Montaigne laughed, and I learned how quickly

it is possible to hate. For the laugh cut like a dagger, sharp on both edges. *You are wrong, Papa,* I thought. *Paul de la Montaigne isn't dumb at all.* He was smart in a way my father would never understand. Smart in the ways of giving pain.

"Why, Belle, of course," he answered. "After all, you must know what they say."

For a fraction of a second, Celeste's gaze shifted so that her eyes looked back straight into mine. "Well, yes, of course I do," she said, her eyes back on Paul de la Montaigne once more. "But I would so love to hear *you* say it."

Paul de la Montaigne smiled. "Why, that she is the living embodiment of her name! That's the reason she never goes out in public, because she's so Beautiful, too Beautiful for all but a few privileged pairs of eyes to gaze upon."

Suddenly, I felt cold all over, not just in my limbs but in my very soul.

"And naturally you're hoping yours will be one of those pairs," my sister said evenly.

"Well, of course," Paul de la Montaigne responded. He reached out and captured Celeste's hand. "So tell me: Is it true?"

My heart began to pound in hard and painful strokes.

Turn around and see for yourself was all Celeste needed to say.

She never so much as glanced in my direction. Instead, she gave a laugh like a chime of bright silver bells. "Surely you don't expect me to answer a question like that," she said playfully. As if chastising a naughty child, she reached out to swat

Paul de la Montaigne on one arm. "You don't give away your family's secrets, do you?"

"Of course not."

"Then why should you expect me to give away mine?"

Celeste got to her feet, carefully gathering her silk skirts before Paul de la Montaigne could reply. As if awakened from a dream, I started, clutched my own skirts in my hand, and darted around the arbor, out of sight.

"And now, if you'll excuse me," I heard Celeste go on, "I really must rejoin my family. Belle is here somewhere, of course. But I wonder if you'll be able to recognize her. Beauty is not always what you expect, you know."

With her head held high, my sister walked out of the rose garden. I waited until a frowning Paul de la Montaigne had departed as well before leaving my hiding place. Any pleasure I'd felt that day had been completely spoiled.

Never before had I been used by another to inflict pain on somebody I loved. More than anything in the world, I wished I had been brave enough to confront Paul de la Montaigne myself. But I was not.

And it would be a very long time, I thought, before I banished the image of Celeste turning her own Beauty into a mask to hide her wounded heart.

Eight

THE EVENTS OF THE DE LA MONTAIGNE GARDEN PARTY
marked a change in our household, though I don't think any of
us realized how great a change at the time. The unhappiness, the
sense of good intentions gone awry, came home with us and
took up permanent residence. It became one of us.

My mother did not make me go out again. Paul de la
Montaigne's name was no longer mentioned in our house.
When I tried to express my appreciation to Celeste for what
she'd done, she simply turned and walked away. But whether
this was because she was angry with me or found the subject
too painful to revisit, I could not tell.

Even the weather seemed out of sorts. That summer was

the hottest any of us could remember—fierce, blazing weather, so blistering some days that not so much as a breath of air seemed to be stirring. We could not sit outdoors at all, not even in the shade of the large oak tree in the yard.

Overnight, storm clouds would appear, sliding silently across the sky, though the wind that blew them never seemed to touch the ground. The clouds would hunker down for days, thick and black, as if determined to choke out the sky. On those days, the air would become so thick with moisture that breathing became an effort. But it refused to rain. Instead, we'd wake up one morning to find the storm clouds had gone and the scorching sun was back.

And so that long, strange summer turned into a tense and troubled autumn.

The signs that something serious was going on were small at first. Papa went to his shipping office at the waterfront each morning and returned each evening with a furrowed brow. But slowly, as autumn changed to winter, the frown became a permanent addition to my father's face, and he no longer went to his workshop after the regular day's work was done.

Instead, Papa and Grand-père Alphonse spent their evenings together, poring over sea charts. At night, as my sisters and I lay in bed, we could hear our parents' voices melding together—Papa's calm and steady; Maman's rising sharply, then abruptly falling silent. It didn't take a fortune-teller or a genius to read these signs.

Something was terribly wrong.

Papa's ships weren't returning as expected. It was as if the weather that had so affected us was affecting all the globe. Usually, most of my father's fleet of merchant vessels was safe in port by now. For soon it would be winter, the time to make repairs and plan for the new year. But without ships, without even knowledge of their whereabouts, Papa could make no plans for the future. Even worse, unable to sell the missing ships' cargoes, my father could generate no income.

If it had been only a few ships that did not return, we might have managed. Shipping is a risky business even in the best of times. And my father is a careful man, always cautious not to overextend himself. But this was different—not a portion of that on which our livelihood depended, but all of it. A disaster so large, it was impossible to plan for.

If Papa had been a different sort of man, a greedy man, all might still have gone well for us. But he was not. My father felt keenly his responsibility to the families of the men who sailed for him, families who often struggled to make ends meet despite the decent wages paid to them by LeGrand, Delaurier and Company. Had not my father been a poor man, a poor sailor's son? He would not let the families of his men struggle while his own family lived in luxury. For the truth was, they stood to lose far more than we did: fathers, husbands, sons.

First, Maman began to sell her jewelry. I gladly added the buckles that had so plagued my feet to the pile. The forks, knives, and spoons we'd always saved for company came next, ed shortly thereafter by the everyday silver. We sold the paintings in their gilded frames off our walls, the dresses from out of our wardrobes. None of us went out now. But nothing we relinquished quite equaled our financial responsibilities. It was as if we were pouring our money and possessions into a dark and bottomless hole.

Finally, only the house, our horses, and a few cherished possessions remained. I still remember that evening when Papa called us into the dining room. We still had a dining room table, though the elaborately carved sideboard and its contents of silver serving dishes, crystal, and china were gone. Papa had sold them to Henri de la Montaigne just that morning. Then Papa and I had spent the afternoon distributing the proceeds among the families of the men aboard Dominic Boudreaux's ship, the *April Dawn*.

Beside me at the table, April's eyes were teary. She claimed it was her sorrow at having to part with our belongings, but I think we all knew that it was something more. Dominic had been a frequent visitor to our home before he sailed away on this last voyage, and, though he had paid my parents all the proper respect, the real purpose for his visits was clear enough. The fact that April returned Dominic's affection was equally clear, though Dominic had not spoken to my father before he sailed, and April had kept her feelings to herself. Naturally, this made it all the more difficult to offer her comfort.

"Girls," my father said, "your mother and I have been talking things over. . . ."

I think Papa would have reached out to hold Maman's hand for comfort if he could have, but we were sitting in our usual places: Maman and Papa at either end of the long table, Celeste, April, and I in between them.

Maman's eyes were red. But her face looked determined and calm. The last few months had wrought a change in my mother. After the initial shock, Maman had weathered the sale of nearly all the fine things she'd once so treasured and the snubbing by those she'd once considered friends. Her fortitude was nothing short of inspirational. I think even she had been surprised to discover that, beneath all her fine satins and silks, my mother possessed a backbone of iron.

"It's the house, isn't it?" I asked.

My father nodded. "I'm sorry to say it," he said, "but the house must be sold. I had a letter from Alphonse this morning." He let his fingers rest on an envelope in front of him. Grand-père Alphonse had been gone for at least a week, on an errand whose purpose I was just now beginning to comprehend.

"He writes that he has found us a place in the country," my father went on. "We will move by the end of the month."

"Are the ships all lost then, Papa?" April asked, her voice no more than a thin ribbon of sound. "Have we given up hope?"

"Of course not," my father said at once, though the weariness and sadness were plain in his voice. "It is never a good idea to abandon hope."

"But hope is not the same as a ship safely returned to port, is it?" April continued softly. "Hope does not reunite your sailors with those who love them, with those they love."

"No," my father answered steadily as he met April's gaze. "It does not. But it does teach us not to despair. It gives us something to hold on to, until word comes of what has happened.

"All may yet be well. I pray for this with all my heart. But I cannot run a business on hopes and prayers, even if my bankers would allow it. I have tried to put this day off for as long as possible, but . . ."

"Where is this new house, Papa?" Celeste inquired.

"A day and a half's journey inland," my father said. "One day through the Wood, and another half day beyond. Alphonse writes that of all the places he saw, this is the one he thinks will suit us best, and I am willing to trust his judgment."

Papa's gaze roamed around our spacious dining room. "It will be smaller than what we're used to, of course," he said, almost as an afterthought. "But Alphonse says that the house itself is well-made and snug. The land has a stream and there is a barn for the horses and for livestock."

"But if there is no money, how will we pay for a new place to live?" Celeste asked.

My father cleared his throat, as if the words were stuck there and he had to force them out.

"Alphonse has sold his own house," Papa replied. "He will see us safely settled in the country, then return to the city and live in the rooms above the office."

"Oh, but—" Celeste began, then stopped abruptly. The question she'd kept herself from asking still hung in the air: If Grand-père Alphonse could stay in town, why couldn't we all stay?

"We cannot afford it," my mother spoke up. "One person can live in the city much less expensively than five."

I saw her look down the length of the table to meet my father's eyes. "Making a clean break is the best thing, for all of us," she continued. "And as your father says, all may yet be well."

But in the present, things were far from well. We spent the rest of that month packing those belongings we felt we could not live without. On the first day of February, we set out for our new home.

Nine

HAVE YOU EVER HAD SOMETHING SO MOMENTOUS AND unexpected happen that it makes you reconsider all the things you used to agonize over?

That's what moving to the country did for me. Whether or not my name was the true match for my face just didn't seem so important anymore.

This is hardly to say I set off for the country with a brave heart, however. How could I? I was leaving behind everything I'd loved, everything familiar.

But no matter what you do to postpone it, the future always shows up at your door. The fact that our door was changing wouldn't make one bit of difference.

We got up early on the morning of our departure. It would be a day and a half of travel overall, according to my father. And we knew the first day's travel would be the longest, for we must be clear of the Wood by nightfall.

I should probably explain about the Wood, shouldn't I?

In fact, considering the importance it came to have for all of us, most especially for me, perhaps I should have mentioned it long before now. But that would have been cheating, putting the middle and end of my story before its start. Introducing you to it now means we enter the Wood together.

The town of my birth looks out toward the sea, curving as if in one slow smile along the coastline. But at its back, snuggled up against it like a cat seeking warmth in winter, lies a great green swath. For as long as anyone can remember, people have simply called it "the Wood." You can traverse it in a day if you go straight through, but it takes three whole days to ride around it.

In spite of this difference, most travelers take the long way around. You can probably guess why. There are tales about what happens beneath the boughs of the Wood—as many as there are trees in the Wood itself. Growing up, my sisters and I heard many of them. Tales of the Wood were our second-favorite bedtime stories, just after the ones we had once made up ourselves about Monsieur LeGrand.

There was the tale of a stand of trees with bark as pale as pearls and leaves of such a color that, when they fell from the branches in autumn, it was like watching a shower of the finest gold. The nursemaid who told us this claimed if you found these trees and stood beneath them as the wind blew, you would come away with your pockets filled with golden coins.

We heard of places in the Wood where the snow fell all year long, sweet as sugar on the tongue, and places where winter never came at all. Places filled with the voices of birds too numerous to count and places where it was so quiet that you could hear the sap run and the trees themselves grow taller.

And finally there were the tales of the Wood's dark places, tales that kept us up at night, tales that could only be told in a whisper, for to speak them any louder might invite the dark into the room with you. It goes without saying that my sisters and I loved these tales the best.

And the one we loved the very most, which kept us from falling asleep the longest, was the tale of a monster dwelling in the most secret heart of the Wood.

It was no ordinary monster, of course. This monster could command the elements. Bend time so as to never grow old. Shape light and dark, becoming visible or invisible at will. The only thing the monster could not do was no doubt the thing it wanted most: It could not leave the Wood.

This last part was all that kept Celeste, April, and me from complete and utter terror. As it was, the first time we heard the tale of the monster in the Wood, we lay awake for three nights running. On the fourth day, Maman dismissed the nursemaid who'd seen fit to tell us the story in the first place. It was Papa who tucked us into bed that night, and as he did so, he soothed away our fears.

It's not so much that what they say is truthful, Papa assured us in his quiet, steady voice, but that certain kinds of stories have the ability to teach us truths about ourselves. There was no real monster living in the heart of the Wood. Rather, the story was a way to think about the monster that might dwell in our own hearts. *That* was the monster we should fear the most, or so my father said.

Papa's explanation made it easier to fall asleep at night, but I wasn't altogether sure I accepted it.

Any child can tell you that monsters are as real as you and I are. So why shouldn't the tales be true? Why shouldn't there be a monster dwelling in the Wood's most secret heart? Such a hidden place seemed as fine as any for a being bound by rules of enchantment, but not those that fettered the rest of us, to call his home.

And now you know as much about the Wood as I did when I first set foot beneath its boughs.

On the first day of our journey, we set off long before the sun was up. It felt a strange, unnatural time to be leaving, as if we were beginning our new life before the old one was truly over. But it had been both of my parents' choice. Neither of them wished to attract a crowd, I think, even of well-wishers, and certainly not those who pitied us or would gloat over our misfortune. It was better to slip away quietly, though not so quickly as to seem like we were running away.

Winding our way through the city streets, the jangle of harnesses and the steady clop of our horses' hooves on the cobblestone were the only sounds. After a time, we reached the stone wall that wraps around the town like outstretched arms. There are gates set into the wall at regular intervals so that no one from the outside can sneak up on the city.

Neither my sisters nor I had ever left the protection of the city walls. We did so now, in single file. Just as my horse stepped through the gate, the sun came up. I pulled back on the reins in surprise.

For instead of the blue of the ocean to which I was accustomed, I found myself looking out into a waving sea of green, flecked with rose and gold. And so it was that I saw the Wood for the very first time, while it looked to hold the greatest promise: at dawn.

Unexpectedly, I felt my heart lift. *Perhaps Papa is right,* I thought. *Perhaps all may yet be well after all.*

Then I put my heels to my horse and followed my family toward whatever lay in store.

"Where is the heart of the Wood, Grand-père Alphonse?" I asked several hours later. "Do you know?"

Out of the corner of my eye, I thought I saw him smile.

The two of us were now riding at the head of the party,

instead of bringing up the rear in single file as we had been before. Beyond the city gate, the narrow streets of the city opened out into a great causeway that ran the length of the wall, making it easier for the large wagons of trade caravans to navigate. Something about all that space just plain went to my head, as far as I can tell.

Having spurred my horse on once, I had done so again, moving forward to the front of the line. Hardly my usual position, but why shouldn't I go first? We were beginning a new life. Surely, the old order of things need not apply.

It was exciting to feel the wind in my face and to know my eyes were the first to gaze upon whatever was to come. After a few moments, Grand-père Alphonse joined me, for even once we entered the Wood, the path stayed broad enough for two to travel side by side. Besides that, it made good sense for Grand-père Alphonse to take the lead. He was the only one who actually knew where we were going.

Not that any of us could have gotten lost. The path ran as straight as that of an arrow. The trees grew so close along the roadway that I could have reached out and brushed them with my fingertips. I inhaled deeply, tasting the sharp scent of pine at the back of my throat.

"You are thinking of the story," Grand-père Alphonse said.

"I suppose I am," I answered with a smile. "Perhaps I'm simply being childish. We've heard dozens of stories over the years, but I never thought I'd actually set foot inside the Wood itself. That makes the tales feel . . . different, somehow."

"I know just what you mean," Grand-père Alphonse said with a nod. "I felt the same way myself, the first time I came here, as if all the tales were going to come to life around me."

"Well, if they're going to do that," Celeste piped up behind us, "why not look for the grove that rains down golden coins? If we gathered some of those, we could go back home where we belong."

"I didn't say I wanted to find the heart of the Wood," I said into the charged silence that followed my sister's words. There was no home to go back to, even if we could. After all that had happened, who was to say where we belonged?

"I only asked Grand-père Alphonse if he knew where it was."

"I do not," Grand-père Alphonse said simply. He twisted in his saddle to look back at Celeste. "And I think that we are safe enough, Celeste. No road leads to the heart of the Wood, as far as I know. It is a place that gives up its secrets only when it chooses. That's what I've heard said, anyhow."

"Well, I, for one, hope it keeps them to itself," remarked my mother as Grand-père Alphonse faced forward again. "Things are bad enough without monsters popping out to frighten us."

As if the Wood understood her words, a sudden wind swept through the trees, followed by an absolute stillness, which even momentarily muffled the sounds of our horses' hooves.

"I think," my father said carefully, "that we have had quite enough talk of monsters."

We rode in silence for a while. I kept my eyes trained on the path, each one of my senses heightened.

"There is another tale of the Wood that I could tell you, if you like," Grand-père Alphonse offered, breaking the uncomfortable silence that had fallen upon us all. "One that I think will appeal to you especially, Belle."

Celeste gave an unladylike snort. "In that case, it must be about a piece of wood."

I swiveled in my saddle to stick out my tongue.

"As a matter of fact, you're right," Grand-père Alphonse answered with a chuckle. "But there's something in it for you, too, Celeste, for it's also a tale of love."

"That would make it a tale for April, then," Celeste contradicted.

"That will do, Celeste," my mother interjected. "What is this tale that you would tell us, Alphonse?"

"It is the story of the Heartwood Tree. Do you not know it?"

"I do not," replied Maman.

"Well, I will tell it to you," Grand-père Alphonse said. And this is the tale that he told us as we rode.

Ten

"ONCE UPON A TIME THERE LIVED A YOUNG HUSBAND AND wife. Though they had been married less than a year's time, it seemed they had known each other forever, for they had been childhood sweethearts and loved each other almost all of their lives.

"The couple often took walks beside a glistening lake, and when they paused to look at their reflections in the water, even as their eyes beheld two individual people, they felt they were seeing just one being, so closely were their two hearts joined."

"So this *is* a tale of true love, then," April spoke for the first time.

"It is," Grand-père Alphonse agreed, his eyes fixed on the

road ahead. "And so I would like to tell you this couple lived happily ever after. That they lived long and prosperous lives together. But they did not.

"Not long after their wedding, the wife became sick with an illness that had no cure. She grew very frail and died in her husband's arms. His grief was so intense that it caused others pain to behold it, for there is something truly terrible about a love that is snatched away too soon."

Grand-père Alphonse paused to take a breath, and in the silence I could almost hear Dominic Boudreaux's name whispered through the treetops. Had he met a watery grave? I yanked myself back to the present at the sound of Grand-père Alphonse's voice.

"The young widower chose his wife's gravesite with great care," Grand-père Alphonse continued. "He buried her beside the lake where they had so loved to walk. And over her heart, he planted her favorite tree: a pink-blossomed dogwood.

"When this was done, the young man sat down upon the grave that now contained all he held dear, and wept for eight full days and seven full nights until his heart was empty and his eyes were dry.

"And then the young man put his head down on the earth, just as he had once set it on the pillow beside his wife's, and went to sleep, no longer caring if he awoke the next morning."

"What a strange, sad story this is, Alphonse," commented my mother.

"It is," Grand-père Alphonse said with a nod. "But it is also full of wonder. For on the eighth night, as the young man slept, a strange event transpired. The dogwood tree took root, then grew into something else entirely.

"For it was a tree unlike any other: nurtured by the bones of true love below it, and watered by the tears of heartfelt grief above it. And so, when the new day dawned, and the widower opened his eyes, he found himself lying beneath the boughs of a ten-foot tree.

"As he gazed upon it, the tree burst into bloom, and its branches bore flowers such as no one had ever seen before. Some carried blooms of a white more pure than winter's first snowfall, while others bore those as red as freshly spilled blood.

"Though startled, the young man understood at once: The white blossoms were the symbol of his grief, sprung from the bones of his beloved. And the red were the symbol of his love, borne from his own heart.

"No sooner did he comprehend this than a wind came up, streaming through the branches over his head, raining petals down upon him. As they mingled together, the petals formed a third color: a pink precisely the same shade as the first blush of dawn.

"The widower rose to his feet, gathered as many of the soft, delicate petals as he could, and set off for home. There, he placed them in a clear glass jar and set the jar on the windowsill beside his bed, so the petals would be the first thing he would see when he awoke each morning.

"One new day dawned, and then another, and so, first days, then weeks, then months, and, finally, years went by. But no matter how much time passed, the petals always remained true and never faded.

"And in this way, the husband was comforted. For it seemed to him that, though he could no longer hear her laughter, no longer reach out and take her by the hand as he had once so loved to do, his wife had not completely left him. Her love still kept pace with his. It still walked the earth beside him though she could not.

"Her love was in the sound of the wind as it danced through the treetops, the sound the brook made, running swift and high. It was in the busy talk of chickadees on a cold morning and the call of a single raven just at nightfall. But most of all, it was in the petals in the jar on the windowsill—petals that retained the same color as the day he had first gathered them.

"And so he called the tree that had started as one thing but blossomed into another, the Heartwood Tree. And he decreed that no one must cut its boughs. For, like love, the gifts the Heartwood has to offer cannot be forced. They must be given freely, or not at all. For anything less is no true gift.

"The man never married again, but spent his days living quietly by the lakeside. When he died peacefully in his sleep, he was buried beneath the Heartwood Tree, alongside his wife. Never once, in all those years, did the tree shed more than its petals. All heeded the young widower's words, none daring to cut the Heartwood's limbs.

"For it is whispered that when the Heartwood Tree gives itself at last, letting loose a branch of its own accord, it will be to one with the heart to see what lies within the wood. To see what the husband and wife grew together out of their joy and sorrow combined: the face of true love."

We rode for some distance, none of us speaking. But the Wood around us was far from silent. It seemed to whisper secrets to itself.

"I told you it was going to be a story about wood," Celeste said at last, breaking the long silence.

"Oh, Celeste," April protested, but I could hear the laughter in her voice.

I laughed too, though my heart was beating as if I'd run all the way from town. I knew why Grand-père Alphonse had told the story. What better hands for a piece of the Heartwood Tree to fall into than my own?

If only such a tale were true, I thought. *If I could hold a piece of Heartwood in my hand, then I might see the face inside it. The face of the one person who would see me as I am, Beautiful or not, and cherish me for it.*

My true love.

"Oh, Celeste's just afraid the tree wouldn't share its secrets with her," I teased. "Or if it did, it would be by a branch falling on her head."

"Well, maybe that's how it works," April said. "The branch conks you on the head, and then you see visions."

"You two are absolutely impossible," Celeste cried. She kicked her heels against her horse's flanks, urging him forward, through the narrow gap between Grand-père Alphonse and me.

"Oh, no you don't!" I called. "I like being first, and I intend to stay there."

"You'll have to catch me, too, then!" April suddenly exclaimed as she followed Celeste's example.

I thumped my heels against my horse's sides again. And so, inspired by a story of loss and redemption, my sisters and I raced toward whatever the future might bring.

We left the Wood just at nightfall.

Eleven

THE SECOND PART OF OUR JOURNEY WAS SWIFT, FOR THE road continued fine and even and soon brought us into the countryside. The landscape was one of tiny valleys nestled between gently rolling hills. The hills would be a soft golden color in the summer, Grand-père Alphonse told us. At the moment they were covered with light green fuzz, which would turn into a green so bright it would bring tears to our eyes. Or so Grand-père Alphonse promised, anyway.

Half a day's travel along the winding country road brought us, at last, to our new home.

Papa had said there was a stream on our new land, and we heard it long before we ever saw it. At first, it was no more than a teasing whisper of water, always just out of sight, as if it were playing hide-and-seek with us. But soon we caught glimpses of it snaking through the hills. Gradually, it grew closer, and the whisper became a murmur and, finally, a pure, clear song of liquid flowing over stones.

The stream greeted us as we rounded the bend and the view opened up. The house that was to be our new home was some distance from the main road, though plainly visible from it, nestled against the base of a small hill. The stream flowed toward the house, then made a quick, darting curve behind it, as if hurrying to get wherever it was going. The barn sat to one side of the house.

The house itself was faced in weathered gray shingles and had a roof of sod. I had never seen such a thing before. The front windows sparkled in the midday sunlight and between them, in an unexpected burst of color, was a bright blue door.

For several moments, no one spoke.

"It doesn't have a dirt floor, does it?" Celeste inquired.

"Oh, for heaven's sake, Celeste," my mother exclaimed.

"It's not that far-fetched," my sister protested. "There's grass on the roof."

"That is an old trick," said Grand-père Alphonse. "It helps keep the house warm in the winter and cool in the summer. There's hay in the walls for the same reason."

"It looks a snug and cheerful place," my father said.

"I hope that you will find it so," Grand-père Alphonse

replied. "But to answer your question, Celeste, the floors are made of wood."

"Thank goodness for that," my sister said. "At least there will be something that I recognize."

"Oh, hush, Celeste," I said as I swung down from my horse. "You're not being clever, just unhelpful."

Grand-père Alphonse dismounted, then turned and held one hand up to my oldest sister.

"She is nervous," he said calmly. "Which is perfectly reasonable. Come inside, all of you, and see your new home."

Grand-père Alphonse stayed several weeks, helping us unpack and arrange our belongings—the few treasures we could not bear to leave behind—and grow accustomed to our new surroundings.

Maman still had her favorite chair, the one in which she sat to work her fancy embroidery. This was placed in the room to the left of the short set of central stairs, for Maman had decreed that this would be the living room. Though, when you got right down to it, the room on the right would have done just as well, for the two rooms were precisely the same size. We had discovered almost at once that our new home had been built along strict symmetrical lines.

Maman's chair went nearest the fireplace, with the great, round freestanding hoop for holding her linen to the right of the chair, and the basket that held her needles and skeins of silk on the left. Papa had made them both as a gift for their first anniversary, many years ago.

April brought with her an elaborately carved chest of sandalwood that had been a gift from Dominic following his first voyage as captain of the *April Dawn*. I had no idea if it was empty, or if she had placed other treasures inside. Celeste had her dressing table with its stool of padded silk, and the ivory-backed brushes with which she gave her hair its one hundred and one strokes both morning and night.

As for me, I had a chest, as well, fashioned of hemlock wood. I had made it myself. After it was finished, I had rubbed it gently with linseed oil to make it shine. Hemlock is a soft wood, so the chest had to be treated carefully, but I loved its golden color.

Inside the chest, I had carefully placed the canvas bundle that contained my carving tools, some treasured pieces of uncarved wood, and as many of my father's woodworking tools as the chest would hold. Grand-père Alphonse and I had schemed together on this, for Papa had decided that, now that he would be without his workshop, he would leave behind all but his most basic carpentry tools.

But I knew how important it was to Papa to work with his hands. I simply could not imagine him without a project of some kind. And I was afraid that, without a task to occupy his hands and mind, my father would worry himself into an illness, for I had only to look at him to see how the last few months had taken their toll.

At the back of the first floor, behind the central stair, were two more rooms, a kitchen and a pantry. The upstairs was divided into two long, narrow rooms that ran from the front of the house to the back, as opposed to the downstairs rooms, which were side to side.

One of these would serve as a bedroom for my parents, the other, for my sisters and me. Maman had actually given us permission to place our beds in whatever position we liked, though we had selected our places in order of birth. Old habits are hard to shake.

Celeste placed her bed in the center of the long wall that divided the two rooms, with her dressing table alongside. April tucked hers under the eaves. That left me to place mine precisely where I would have chosen, had I been allowed to go first: beneath the center window along the outside wall. During the day, I could look out and see the hills rolling away toward the Wood. At night, I could look out and see the stars.

Those first weeks, we kept busy, putting all thoughts of the city resolutely from our minds as we moved furniture and supplies, arranging and rearranging them as we learned how to make this strange new house our own.

It was Papa and Grand-père Alphonse, both of whom had grown up without servants, who showed the rest of us how to build a fire in the wood stove in the kitchen, how to bank it at night so that it would not go out, and then how to stoke it up once more the following morning.

I learned to tell—by how fast water dried on my hand—whether the oven was a fast oven, hot enough to bake a pie, or had cooled down enough to be called medium, just right for bread or rolls. Last was the slow oven to be used for things like custard, which would curdle if it got too hot too fast, but which could stay in a cooler oven for a long time.

Celeste caught on to this the quickest and soon assumed most of the cooking duties, much to all of our surprise, including, I think, her own. She had always been clever. This much, we knew, for all too often we had felt her cleverness through her sharp tongue.

But I don't think it had once occurred to any of us that part of Celeste's sharpness might have been because she was bored by what our old life had to offer. To me it had seemed as if my oldest sister had always had the life she wanted, though all it asked of her was that she be Beautiful. And this she could do as easily as breathing; it took no thought or effort at all. Now it was as if working in the kitchen gave Celeste a purpose, a reason to be clever, where she'd had none before.

While Celeste took on the cooking, April and I struggled to master the rest of the tasks needed to keep a household running, for we were determined to spare Maman as much of the heavy work as possible. She protested at this until Papa remarked how much lovelier the downstairs rooms would look with new curtains at the windows, and, personally, he'd always been very fond of embroidered ones.

That was all it took to get Maman to settle right to work making some. This left April and me free to take on the remainder of the chores, all of which seemed to involve mopping, dusting, or scrubbing. By the end of the very first week, I had a whole new appreciation for Marie Louise, the housekeeper we'd had to leave behind in the city, as well as all the maids we'd employed.

Now it was April's turn to surprise us, for no task seemed too difficult or dirty for her. The more challenging the task, the more she seemed to like it, in fact. It was almost as if she wanted to wear herself out, so that she wouldn't have the energy to worry about Dominic—though this was pure supposition on my part, as she still refused to speak of him at all.

With Celeste mastering the kitchen and April the cleaning, I worked outdoors with Papa and Grand-père Alphonse. Together, we laid out a plot for a kitchen garden. It was still too early, the ground too cold, to plant the seeds that we had brought. But at least I could get a head start on deciding where they'd go.

After Papa, Grand-père Alphonse, and I had laid out the garden, we went to work refurbishing the barn. It was as well-made as the house, so this was mostly a matter of getting the horses settled into their new homes.

But at the very back, in a space that had once been a tack room, I did my best to create a new workshop for Papa. This was a tricky task, as I had to do it on the sly. The rest of the family was in on the secret, of course. Everyone helped to keep Papa distracted and out of the way. Grand-père Alphonse turned out to be the greatest help.

You could live in the city without knowing who your neighbors were, he said. But in the country, it was a good idea to at least know *where* they were, in case you needed to ride for help. So, while Celeste mastered the kitchen, Maman the curtains, and April the rest of the house in general, Grand-père Alphonse took Papa farther into the countryside.

It felt strange and lonely to be in a new place without him, but it *did* give me time to complete my surprise, and the new workshop was ready the day they returned. Grand-père Alphonse would begin the trip back to the city the following morning.

"Papa," I said as I came into the kitchen. It was early evening, not quite time for dinner, and Papa was sitting at one end of the table drinking a mug of tea. At the other end of the table, Celeste was busy peeling potatoes.

"I'm sorry to bother you," I went on. "But there's something I need your help with in the barn."

Celeste met my eyes swiftly, a look of question in them. I nodded my head ever so slightly. Celeste turned her attention back to the potatoes.

"You can see that Papa is having his tea, Belle," she remarked. "Couldn't your problem at least wait until he's done?"

She sounded so precisely like her old cross self that I bit the inside of my cheek to keep from smiling.

"I didn't say there was a problem," I replied. "I only said I needed him to come and look at something."

Papa pushed back from the table. "I can do that easily enough," he said. "The tea will still be here when I get back."

Celeste dropped a potato into a pot of cold water with a *plop* and said nothing more.

"I *am* sorry to make you get up," I said to my father as we walked toward the barn, side by side. "I know you must be tired."

"I am, a little," my father replied. He gave the seat of his pants a rub, a rueful expression on his face. "I'm afraid I'm not cut out to be much of a rider. I'm happy to stretch my legs a bit, to tell you the truth.

"Now," my father continued briskly as he pushed open the barn's great sliding door, "what is so important that you must interrupt my tea for help?"

"It's back here," I said as I led the way. "I've wanted to ask about this ever since you left. I'm just not sure I've set up this room quite right."

I reached the room I'd worked so hard to keep secret, lifted the latch, and pushed open the door, gesturing for Papa to go in first. I'd left a lantern burning, placing it carefully so that it was safe, and so that it would illuminate as much of the room as possible.

"What do you think?" I asked. "Did I do a good job?"

My father took several steps forward, then stopped abruptly.

He pivoted in a complete circle on one heel, without making a single sound. But I saw the way his eyes moved around the room, taking in all the details. It was as close to his workshop in town as I could make it.

"You did this?" he said finally.

I nodded. "With Grand-père Alphonse's help. With everyone's help, actually, for they all kept you busy."

My father let out a long, slow breath. Until that moment, I hadn't realized I'd been holding mine.

"Thank you, Belle," he said. "I have tried not to be selfish, but I admit it gave me a pang to leave my workshop behind."

"You are the least selfish person I know," I said. "A selfish man would not have given up his fine city house to care for the wives and children of sailors."

"Ah, but you forget," my father answered quietly. "I am a sailor's child. Without Alphonse, I'd have had no fine things to give away." He moved to me, and put an arm around my shoulders. "Like him, you have given me something that costs you very little, but counts for much."

I leaned against him, putting my head on his shoulder. "And what is that?" I asked.

"Kindness," said my father. He dropped a kiss on the top of my head. "Now, let's go back inside. I think Celeste is making something special for Alphonse's last night with us."

With his arm still around my shoulders, my father and I walked back to the house.

Twelve

GRAND-PÈRE ALPHONSE DEPARTED THE NEXT DAY, RIDING out shortly after noon, beneath a cloudy sky. He promised to let us know the moment there was reliable word on any of Papa's ships. Our tiny new house felt large and empty after he was gone. And, though we had been working hard at many different things, Grand-père Alphonse's return to the city marked the true beginning of our new lives.

Our days soon fell into a rhythm, each day with its own chore. On Monday, Celeste rose early to bake pies and bread. Tuesday, she sat and sewed with Maman while April and I heated endless kettles of water to do the washing. I quickly grew to dislike washing day. It was exhausting work and my arms and back ached by the time we were done.

Wednesday, Celeste baked again, while April did the ironing and I worked outdoors.

In addition to the patch for vegetables, Papa and I were digging flower beds, particularly outside the window of the room where Maman sat and sewed. The gardens in our yard in the city had been her pride and joy. She'd brought blossoms indoors every day when the weather was fine.

While I'd been busy preparing a surprise for Papa, April had been saving one for Maman: The trunk April had brought with her was filled with rose cuttings, one from every bush Maman had had to leave behind. At the rate things were warming up, I'd be able to plant them soon. For, though our days were often damp and chilly, we were well on our way to spring.

And we'd discovered the reason the hills around us turned a green so intense it brought tears to the eyes. It was because, during early springtime, the weather drizzled almost nonstop.

"I think I'm beginning to grow mold," I remarked late one afternoon as I came into the kitchen. For once, it wasn't raining, but was still wet and muddy outdoors. "Maybe that's why the hills get so green. They're moldy too."

Celeste opened the oven door and peered inside. It was the first day of April, our own April's birthday. Celeste was baking a cake, her first, as a surprise.

"You take those muddy shoes off before you set one foot in this kitchen, Belle Delaurier," she said without turning around.

"Thank you for the reminder," I said tartly. Celeste may have gotten easier to live with, but she was still bossy. I sat down on the chair that was kept just inside the door for precisely the purpose of removing muddy shoes, though I made no move to take mine off.

"This may come as a surprise to you, old and wise as you have become, but I do know better than to track mud all over the floor."

"Who's old and wise?" April asked as she came into the room. She had a big apron tied over her dress. It was her afternoon to do the dusting, a task she'd refused to relinquish, birthday or not.

"Celeste," I replied.

April's eyebrows shot up. "When did all this happen?" she inquired.

"I'd be careful, if I were you," Celeste remarked. She set the pan with the cake at the back of the stove with a *clank*. Apparently, it was done. "Remember who cooks the meals around here."

"But never does the washing up," I replied. That task usually fell to me these days. My one consolation was that it helped keep my hands clean. No matter how careful I was to wear gloves, I always seemed to end up with dirt under my nails from working in the garden.

"Well, of course not," Celeste said, in a tone that told me this should have been obvious.

April shot me a quick wink.

"Of course not," she echoed.

Without warning, Celeste whirled around, the towel she'd used to protect her fingers from the hot cake pan still in her hands. She wadded it up into a ball and tossed it straight at April. April dodged aside. The towel hit the wall behind her, then slid to the floor.

"Thank you very much," April said. "That's one more thing for me to wash."

"It's not my fault," Celeste said quickly. "I was minding my own business until a few minutes ago." She actually went so far as to point a finger at me. "Blame Belle."

I made a strangled sound of amusement and outrage, both. "What do you mean 'blame Belle'? I didn't do a thing."

"You don't have to *do* anything," Celeste explained, as if I were an idiot. "You're the youngest. You get blamed by default."

"You want something to blame me for?" I inquired.

I stood up. Then I lifted one foot, still in its muddy shoe, and held it beyond the edge of the kitchen mat.

Celeste's eyes narrowed. "You wouldn't *dare*," she said.

"Get mud on my clean kitchen floor and you're mopping it up yourself," April warned.

I brought my foot down, then lifted it straight back up, creating one perfect, muddy footprint.

"That's it," April said. "Now you've done it."

"What do you say we give her *your* birthday spanking right here and now?" Celeste proposed.

"You'll have to catch me first!" I cried out.

I whirled, yanked open the door to the yard, and dashed down the kitchen steps. The clatter of footsteps behind me told me my sisters weren't wasting any time in pursuit. I turned to face them, once again lifting my foot. I held it poised over a very large mud puddle.

"Think carefully before you come any closer," I threatened.

"Go ahead, April. She doesn't really mean it," Celeste said. But we all noticed she'd stopped right where she was.

"Oh, yes, I do," I taunted.

April skidded to a stop beside Celeste. "She says she does."

"Guess there's only one way to find out, isn't there?" Celeste said.

"Guess so."

"No. Wait. Stop!" I cried. But by then it was too late. My sisters had called my bluff. Hands linked, Celeste and April dashed forward, leaped up, and landed full force in the mud puddle.

Water and mud flew in every direction, but mostly, of course, up and out. Within seconds, our skirts were filthy and soaked. I bent down and scooped up two brimming handfuls of mud.

"You're about to be very sorry you did that," I said.

"Look out!" Celeste cried.

I let the mud fly. After that, it was pretty much a free-for-all. I have no idea how long my sisters and I stood in the puddle, shrieking and flinging mud and dirty water at one another. I do know it began to rain at some point. As if this were some previously determined signal, my sisters and I stopped all at once and lifted our filthy faces to the sky.

"If we stand out here long enough, do you think we'll get clean?" April asked after a few moments. She was breathing heavily, as we all were.

I wiped a hand across the front of my dress, leaving behind a trail of mud. "I guess it's not been long enough yet," I remarked.

Celeste laughed first, and before we knew it the three of us were roaring with helpless laughter.

"Well, I guess we all needed that," April remarked. A moment of silence fell. We stood together, our arms around one another.

"I guess we did," Celeste acknowledged. She gazed down at her muddy skirts. "How come we never did things like this before?"

"You've got to be joking," I said. "Can you just see us doing this in town? We'd never have been invited anywhere again."

"You wouldn't have cared about that," Celeste answered. "You never went anywhere anyhow."

I heard April suck in a sudden breath. "No, wait," Celeste said quickly, before anyone else could speak. "I didn't mean it like that. Not sharp, the way it sounded."

"It would be all right even if you did," I answered somberly. "It's true enough." I looked down at my soaked and mud-spattered dress. "I'm not so invisible now, am I?"

"And we're not so very fine and fashionable," April said quietly. "We've only been here a couple of months. How can being in the country have changed us all so much in so little time?"

"Maybe it hasn't," Celeste said. "Maybe this is who we were all along, and we just couldn't see it before. But there aren't so many other eyes to look at us now, are there? Only our own."

"So now the question is," I said, "do we like what we see, or not?"

"What's that?" April interrupted, her head cocked as if she was straining to hear some new sound.

That was the moment I realized I'd been hearing it too, without quite registering what *it* was.

"That's a horse," I said. "Someone's coming."

There was a moment of electric silence. Then, hands still clasped, my sisters and I dashed around to the front of the house. We were just in time to see a single horse leave the main road and start down the one that led to our front door. Its rider swayed in the saddle, clinging to it with both hands, as if this and sheer willpower were the only things keeping him from falling off the horse and into the mud.

"That's not Grand-père Alphonse," Celeste said.

"No," I answered. "It's not. I think maybe it's—"

But by then, April was in motion. Picking up her skirts with both hands, she ran flat out, like a small boy. She reached the horse just as its exhausted rider finally reached our yard. The horse stopped.

"I'm sorry," I heard the horseman say. "I hate to repeat myself. But I'm afraid I'm going to pass out. Again."

Then he pitched sideways in the saddle and slid to the ground just as he had once before, many years ago. April sat down in the mud and cradled his head in her lap.

"Go get Papa," she said. "Go get help."

And then she began to weep the kind of tears no one minds shedding. Tears of joy.

Dominic Boudreaux was home.

Thirteen

"It was the worst possible combination of circumstances," Dominic told us later that night.

We were sitting in the living room, a cheery fire in the grate. All of us had changed out of our filthy, wet clothes. Though in Dominic's case, his only option was to borrow some of Papa's. At my mother's insistence, Dominic was now seated in her chair, the most comfortable in the room. April sat on a low stool beside him. In her hands, she held a mug of steaming broth, from which she urged him to drink from time to time.

Any doubt as to their feelings for each other had been dispelled by the time Dominic and my father staggered through the front door. April had left Dom only long enough for them both to get out of their wet and muddy garments. After that, she'd refused to leave his side.

"What happened?" she asked now.

"It's more a matter of what didn't," Dominic answered, with a tired smile.

First, the *April Dawn* had been blown off course. Then, she'd been becalmed. Seemingly endless days had passed without a stir of air. Food and fresh water had begun to run low. The men had started to fear they would never get home.

"If I'd been sailing for any man but you, Monsieur Delaurier," Dominic said quietly, "been captain of any ship but one of yours, sooner or later I'd have come to a day when I feared for my life. For hungry men become desperate ones in the time it takes to blink, and desperate men commit desperate acts, things they would never consider otherwise."

He paused. April reached up and pressed the mug into his hands. Dominic took a long, slow sip, as if savoring every drop. Papa was a smaller man than Dominic, but Dominic looked thin and frail in Papa's borrowed clothes.

"But the men love you, sir," Dominic went on. "I don't know how to say it any way but that. They know you're a man who honors his word, and sooner than dishonor you, I think they'd have starved. Not one word of mutiny did I hear, and, finally, the wind came back and we made sail for home."

Dominic paused to take another sip of broth, then handed the mug back to April.

"When we finally made port, when we got back and the men learned what you'd done—how you'd sold your own things to care for their families—it was everything I could do to keep them all from coming here with me. There's not one man who won't be willing to set sail again, to look for those lost ships, that is—just as soon as we make repairs to the *April Dawn*."

"Oh, but surely—" April began, then stopped. I could almost see her bite down on her tongue.

"Let's have no more talk of setting sail tonight," my father said into the quick silence that followed April's outburst. "There'll be time enough for that. The men are all well, you say?"

"As well as can be expected, given what they've been though," Dominic replied. "Some will heal faster than others."

"And I imagine good food will soon set most things to rights," my father said.

"True enough, sir," Dominic concurred. "That's true enough."

My father seemed to hesitate, almost as if he wanted to postpone the question we all knew must come next.

"And the cargo?" he finally inquired.

"Safe and sound, every last bit of it," Dominic answered, and I could hear the fierce pride in his voice. "I brought it all home to you, sir. Every last man, every single chest of cargo. It just took a little longer than planned."

All of a sudden, a smile lit Dominic's drawn and tired face.

"Not too bad for the lad who began life as a thief, wouldn't you say?"

"I would," my father replied. He reached out to grip Dom by the arm. "I would indeed say so, and more. You've given back more than you ever tried to take."

"I learned that from you, sir," said Dominic Boudreaux.

My father gave Dominic's arm a final squeeze and then released it, making no attempt to hide the tears that filled his eyes.

"Monsieur LeGrand asked me to tell you you should come without delay, sir, if it can be managed," Dominic went on. "He'd have come himself, but there is much to do."

"That there is," my father said with a smile. "But you have done enough for now. Stay here and rest, Dom. I'll go tomorrow morning. That will put me in the city within two days' time."

Papa left shortly after breakfast the following morning, earlier than he might have when the roads were dry, but the rain continued and, even for a single man on horseback, the going would be muddy and slow. Celeste packed food and water in Papa's saddlebags.

"I cannot promise," my father said as we all stood together in the kitchen, "but if there is money left over after paying off debts, I may be able to bring you something from town. Tell me what you'd like, girls, and I'll do my best to manage it."

"I don't need anything, Papa," April said at once. "Unless there is something that would help Dominic."

As she spoke, the color rose in her cheeks, but she kept her eyes steady on my father's.

"I think food and rest will be enough for him," Papa answered. He reached out and brushed a thumb over one of April's blazing cheeks. "And, of course, your company. I'll expect the two of you to have settled things by the time I return."

He gave April's cheek a sudden pinch, then shifted his attention. "What about you, Celeste?"

"Could you bring some lavender plants, Papa?" my oldest sister asked. "Belle says the cuttings from the rose bushes are almost ready to plant. But if we could have lavender as well . . ."

"You're thinking of your mother," my father said. For though roses were her favorite flower, lavender had always been the fragrance she loved best.

Celeste nodded. "But what would you like for yourself?" my father asked.

Celeste cast her eyes around the kitchen, as if searching for inspiration. "Well, it would be nice to have one more cast-iron skillet," she said. "A really big one."

"A cast-iron skillet," my father echoed.

"I know it would be heavy," Celeste said quickly, as if she'd heard some objection in my father's voice, "but there's Dominic to feed as well now, for as long as he stays, and a bigger pan would be useful, Papa."

"You could always bring sugar, if a new pan is too difficult to carry," I suggested.

Celeste nodded. "Or that, yes. That's a good thought, Belle."

My father put his hands on his hips. "Now, let me see if I have this straight," he said. "My daughters, who not three months past were as fine a collection of fashionable young ladies as anyone could hope to meet, are asking for a pan it takes both arms to lift, and a tonic for a sweetheart? Not one piece of finery among you? Not one ribbon or bow?"

"Well, certainly no buckles," I said, and earned a laugh from everyone present.

"I have no use for fancy ribbons in the kitchen," Celeste said simply. "I'd always be worrying about the ends dragging in the batter or, even worse, catching fire as I work at the stove."

"And they're no good to me when I'm dusting or scrubbing a floor," April chimed in.

"I'll take theirs, Papa," I offered. "I can use it to mark straight rows in the vegetable garden."

"Well," my father said. "Well, then." He stood facing us as we made a little half circle before him. For the second time in as many days, my father had tears in his eyes.

For my sisters and I were sending a message, and my father had heard it, clear as a bell. We would not ask for what we'd valued in our old lives. It would take more than one shipload of cargo to buy those lives back, and I, for one, was far from certain that I wanted mine.

In my old life, I had become invisible. In my new one I was . . . I wasn't quite sure what. But I knew this much: I wanted to find out, for I liked who I was in this new life better than who I'd been before.

But most remarkable was the fact that my sisters and I had each spoken spontaneously. We weren't putting on a brave face we'd discussed ahead of time. We had each spoken truly, from our hearts. We did not want the past. We wanted the future, whatever it might hold.

I don't think I'd ever loved my sisters more than I did in that moment.

"If you're sure," my father said.

"We're sure, Papa," I replied. "Though if you chance to come upon the Heartwood Tree and one of the branches just happens to break off and fall on your head . . ."

My father tossed the saddlebags over one shoulder with a laugh. "I think it's time that I was going. I'll come back as soon as I can. Don't let your mother worry."

"We won't, Papa," April promised.

Together, our arms around one another, my sisters and I crowded into the kitchen doorway, watching until the rain hid my father from view.

And then we began to wait once more.

Fourteen

WE WAITED FOUR LONG WEEKS, UNTIL THE DAYS SLID FROM April into May. At last, the weather turned fine: Glorious spring days filled our hearts with hope for the future.

And so, at last, my father came home.

He arrived at noon, just as Celeste was preparing to set our midday meal on the table. We'd had a brief and unexpected burst of rain that morning, but it had quickly passed, leaving the day sparkling and warm.

Celeste was just taking a fresh-baked pie from the oven when she heard footsteps at the kitchen door. Her cry brought us hurrying in from all parts of the house. Within moments, Papa was seated at the kitchen table, a mug of the tea he so loved close at hand, while Maman, Dominic, and we girls ranged around him.

"It's all right, *mes enfants*," he kept saying over and over. "*I'm all right*."

But it was clear that he was not.

The man who had ridden out to the city four weeks ago had been in high spirits. He'd had a glimmer in his eyes. The man sitting now at the kitchen table was bowed down, as if by some hidden weight almost too great to bear. I'd never seen my father look like this, not even in the days before we'd moved to the country, when each morning brought word of some new loss.

My mother sat beside Papa, an arm around his waist as if to shore him up.

"Drink your tea, Roger," she urged in a soft, firm voice. "You got caught in that rain squall this morning, didn't you? The tea will warm you up."

My father took a sip, obediently, like a child.

"I'm sorry to be such trouble," he said.

"Papa," I said, shocked. "How can you talk so? We love you. How can anything we do for you trouble us?"

The mug of tea slipped from my father's fingers, then bounced off the tabletop and smashed on the floor. Hot liquid and broken crockery shot every which way. None of us moved or made a sound.

Our attention was riveted on my father's face, on the tortured expression in his eyes as they stared into mine.

"Belle," my father said hoarsely, and I felt the hairs on the back of my neck rise at his tone. "*Ma petite Belle.* I wonder if you will say that when you know what I have done."

"I stayed in the city too long. It's as plain as that," my father said some time later. At Maman's urging, we had deferred any explanation of Papa's strange and dire remark until we'd all eaten lunch. If we were about to face some new crisis, she declared, we would need our strength, and no one could be strong on an empty stomach.

Much to my surprise, the food helped—as did the simple act of sitting down and eating together, a family once more. Gradually, the lines in my father's face seemed to ease a little, and his shoulders straightened, though his eyes were still full of worry when he gazed at me from time to time. At last, the meal over, April brewed a fresh pot of tea while Celeste brought out the pie. Then, once more at Maman's urging, Papa began to tell his tale.

"Let me share the good news first," he said, "for there is much that is good to tell. The *April Dawn*'s safe arrival was just the first, Dominic. By the time I reached the city, two more of our ships had arrived at port. This went a fair way toward settling our remaining debts, enough so that my credit is good in the city again and we can begin repairs. Although," my father went on with the ghost of a smile, "I have decided that we will no longer bank with Henri de la Montaigne."

"Good for you, Papa," Celeste said.

Papa drew a deep breath, then let it out. "I stayed in the city longer than I should have," he said again. "But there was so much to accomplish, so much I wanted to see and do. I wanted to visit as many of the men as I could. And then there were the ships to inspect, trying to decide what repairs must be made, when the ships could be ready to sail once more.

"Perhaps I have grown too cautious in my old age," my father went on. "Perhaps I was too anxious to make sure everything would turn out well, that no harm would come to my sailors, or dishonor to us, again."

"But surely no man can truly do that," said my mother.

"You're absolutely right, my dear," my father replied. "At any rate, I realized I'd been gone for nearly four weeks, and, even worse, I'd sent you no word of what was going on. By that time, even Alphonse was urging me to return. I'd been away from all of you quite long enough, he said, and he could manage what still remained to be done."

My father paused to take a sip of tea, as if to fortify himself before continuing.

"So first I stayed too long in the city, and then I left later in the day than I should have. I knew it at the time. But, once I had decided to leave, I felt so eager to be home that even another night away from you seemed too much. And the journey itself was so simple and straightforward. All I had to do was keep to the road. I had been through the Wood twice now. I did not think it held any danger for me.

"But I did not count on the storm."

"What storm, sir?" Dominic asked in the startled silence that followed my father's words. "With the exception of that bit of rain we had this morning, the weather has been fine here the whole time you've been gone."

"You set my mind at ease," my father answered, "strange as that may sound. For the storm I encountered on that night was like none I have ever experienced. It was almost as if it had a will, a mind of its own. As if it sought me out.

"I'd not been in the Wood more than half an hour when it struck. After that, I could not keep track of the time."

"But surely nothing dangerous could happen," Maman said. "As long as you did what you said and stayed on the road."

"That's precisely what I did," my father replied. "But on that day, in that storm, the road led to a place it had not before. I think, perhaps, that this destination was always there, waiting for the right set of circumstances and the right person to come along."

Silence filled the kitchen, but in it was the question that resonated in every mind.

"Where did the road take you, Papa?" I finally asked.

"To the heart of the Wood," my father replied.

Fifteen

"I THINK IT WAS THE WIND THAT DID IT," MY FATHER CON-
tinued. "The wind made it so hard to see where I was going.
For it drove the rain straight into my face, forcing me to bow
my head down. And the sound . . ."

He broke off and shook his head, as if to dispel the memory.

"Not filled with rage, as high winds so often are. But if true
loneliness ever had a voice, it would cry out with the sound of
that wind. Even as it pushed against me, it seemed to pull me
forward.

"I have no idea how long I traveled," my father said. "I
rode until I was soaked clear through to the skin, and my horse
began to stumble. Finally, I got down and led him, fearful that

I'd take a fall and injure myself. But also so that I could feel the road beneath my feet and know that I still traveled on it."

"But you said you never left the road," Celeste countered.

"Nor did I," replied my father. "Remember how we marveled at how smooth and even the surface of the roadway was? The longer I went on, the more it seemed the road began to change beneath my feet, even as I walked along it. It became rough and uneven as if, instead of being well kept up, it had been abandoned, forgotten. It was all I could do to keep my balance.

"In the end, I didn't. My foot turned on a loose stone and I pitched forward, letting go of the horse's reins so that I wouldn't pull him down on top of me. I expected to land flat on my face. Instead, when I reached out to brace myself, my hands found cold, wet metal, and I held on tight.

"I had come to a pair of iron gates."

"You should have turned right around and gone back the other way," my mother announced.

"Maybe," said my father. "But the solution to my situation did not seem so simple at the time. I was wet and I was tired. And, though I don't like to admit it, I was as afraid as I've been in a good long while. Beyond the gates might lie rescue or shelter. Outside them, I knew that there was none.

"So I pushed on the gates. They did not budge. Three times I pushed with all my might, and on the third try, they opened."

"Three," I murmured. "Just like in one of Grand-père Alphonse's stories."

"Even so," my father said with a nod, "for as hard as they'd been to open, those gates swung back without a sound. I gathered the horse's reins and my courage, then walked forward. As we passed through the gates, the storm died down. For the first time in what seemed like hours, I did not have the sound of that terrible wind in my ears.

"I turned back. Through the open gates and beyond them, I could see that the storm still raged. But where I stood, all was still and calm. The path was solid again beneath my feet, and I could see that it was made of stones so smooth and white they looked like polished ivory.

"As I stood hesitating, suddenly unable to decide what I feared more—going forward or turning back—the gates swung closed behind me as silently as they'd opened.

"'That settles that,' I thought. Forward I went, and I did not look back again. I was half convinced the world was unraveling behind me."

"I think you were very brave, Papa," I said.

"Thank you, Belle," my father answered with a tired smile. But when he looked at me, I noticed the sadness still remained in his eyes. There was something he hadn't told yet, the part of the tale that gave him pain.

"Since going forward was my only real choice, I continued to do that," my father went on. "It seemed to me I must have been on the grounds of some great estate. On one side of the road was an orchard of fruit trees, on the other, a garden filled with roses. I could not see their colors in the fading light, but their scent was all around me.

"I'm not sure how long I walked, for I had reached that strange stage of weariness where time seems to fold back upon itself.

"At long last, I came to a short rise, and saw before me a great house made of stone. It seemed to fling itself across the hilltop, as if longing to break free of the constraints of its own construction. To its left sat a row of buildings I thought must be stables. I approached, and found that this was so.

"I stabled my horse, caring for him well and tenderly, for he had been brave that day. Though there were no other horses in the stables, there was food for him in abundance. This reminded me that I was hungry as well. I then approached the house with some trepidation, for I had no idea what I would find inside."

"Oh, but surely you had to know," Celeste interrupted. "The heart of the Wood. That's what you said. So you must have seen the very house of the monster."

"Celeste!" April cried.

"What?" Celeste snapped back, and suddenly the tension in the room ratcheted up sharply. "We're all thinking it. We have been ever since Papa told us that he thought he traveled to the heart of the Wood. Don't get mad at me just because I had the guts to say it out loud."

"Since when do monsters live in houses?" I asked, trying to defuse the situation.

"It's a *monster*," Celeste replied. "Surely that means it can live wherever it wants. Who's going to tell it no? You?"

"Girls," my mother said. "That's enough."

"What *was* inside the house, Papa?" April asked.

"No one," my father replied. "That is to say, no living soul that I encountered. But the front doors parted at my touch as easily as the gates had, and closed behind me just as silently once I had crossed the threshold. Inside, I found myself in a great entry hall. The floor was a mosaic of images beneath my feet, but I did not take time to study the story they might tell.

"I called out, for I did not wish to give offense. There was no reply. Then, as if by way of answer, a door at the hall's far end swung open, and through it, I could see a glow. I called again, and still there was no answer. So, hearing no sound but my own loud breathing and footsteps, I walked the length of the hall until I stood in the open door.

"Before me was what I took to be a small study, for bookcases lined the walls. Directly across from me burned a cheerful fire. This was the glow I had seen from the hall. In front of the fire was a low table set with meat, bread, cheese, and a flagon of wine. A chair was alongside the table, positioned so that its occupant might eat and be warm at the same time.

"I stood in that doorway for I can't tell you how long, till I'd dripped a great puddle of water on the floor and heard my stomach growl. At that, I finally went in, took a seat in the chair, and ate as hearty and delicious a meal as I'd had in my life. Afterward, I slowly drank a glass of wine, the best I'd ever tasted. Before I knew it, the food and wine, combined with my weariness, got the better of me, and I fell asleep before the fire."

"I'd never have been able to do that," April said. "I'd have felt too afraid."

"Did you not feel afraid, sir?" Dominic inquired.

My father was quiet for a few moments. "No, I did not," he answered finally. "It's difficult to explain, but it's almost as if the house felt welcoming. As if it was made peaceful, even joyful, by my presence, and wished to do me good rather than harm."

Papa gazed at us as we sat around the table, holding each of our eyes in turn. "You all know that I am not a fanciful man," my father said. "I have never really believed the old tales of the Wood. To me, they seemed best suited to what they have become: bedtime stories. But I swear to you that I felt something in that house, as if the very stones of which it was made were, themselves, alive. And I felt it welcome me as surely as I felt you welcome me here today.

"But, beneath the welcome, there was something else."

"What was it, Papa?" I asked.

"Loneliness," my father answered. "The silence of that house spoke with the same voice that the windstorm had, with one fierce and endless cry against being alone.

"So, no," my father said once more, turning his gaze again

to Dominic. "I did not feel afraid. If anything, I felt my own good fortune.

"I had been rescued. I was being offered shelter. But in the morning, I would ride away. I could return to my home and those I loved. But the spirit that haunted that place would have no such reprieve. It had to stay behind. I'm not certain how I knew this, but I did. I seemed to feel it in my bones.

"I slept through the night," my father continued. "And awoke refreshed the next morning. My clothes were dry. They bore no trace of having come through a storm, no trace of having been slept in. Nor, for that matter, did I. I wasn't stiff or sore from sleeping in a chair all night. The table beside me had been reset for breakfast. There was fruit and cheese, and a steaming pot of coffee. I breakfasted as well and heartily as I had dined the night before.

"I had half a mind to explore the house, then changed my mind. For the loneliness seemed heavier this morning, as if anticipating my departure, and at that I felt a sharp and sudden longing to be safe in my own home.

"I went to the stable and saddled my horse, who had breakfasted just as well as I. I still had no idea who had provided the food and fresh water, for I neither saw nor heard a single soul.

"'Thank you,' I said to the air in general. I felt slightly foolish, but to go without expressing some thanks did not seem right. 'I don't know who you are, but you have shown me great kindness. I will always honor you for it.' I gathered up the horse's reins and prepared to go.

"As I led the horse from the stable, I caught sight of a smaller path, one I had not noticed in the gloaming the night before. And down the path, I saw a small but beautiful lake with a white pergola near the shore.

"Not far from the pergola, there was a tree in bloom, the loveliest I'd ever seen, or so it seemed, but I could not tell what kind of tree it was. And here, at last, I finally gave in to my curiosity.

" 'What harm can come from going to look at a tree?' I thought. So I left my horse where he stood and went down the hill on foot.

"You will remember I said the house sat at the top of a rise."

"We remember, Papa," I said, nodding.

"The distance was greater than I had thought. Or perhaps it was simply that the closer I came to the tree, the more slowly I walked.

"For as I approached, I began to understand why the tree had caught my eye. The boughs bore blooms of two different colors. Some were a white so pure it was like looking at sunlight on new-fallen snow. Others bore blossoms of a red more rich than any rose. A faint scent filled the air, sweet and promising, like hope.

"Then, as I watched, a faint breeze moved through the branches and a handful of petals released their hold. They tumbled toward the earth, mingling together, and finally came to rest upon the ground below. And there they formed a third color, the soft pink of a new dawn."

I felt a wave of emotion roll through me, so many different things at once I couldn't even begin to identify them all.

"The Heartwood Tree," I said, barely recognizing the sound of my own voice.

"The Heartwood Tree," my father echoed. "As if in a dream, I walked forward until I stood beneath its boughs. I looked up and beheld a fluttering mass of red and white and every variation in between that you can think of. For the petals were in constant motion, like a flock of birds in flight. Where the petals overlapped, new colors formed.

"I have never seen anything so beautiful in my entire life," my father said. "Nor anything so alive. I did not feel the loneliness that had been my constant companion in the house quite so keenly while I was beneath the Heartwood's boughs. Instead I let the sweetness of the air fill up my lungs."

"Papa, please tell me that you didn't," I burst out, unable to contain myself a moment longer. For surely, having come to the Heartwood Tree, we had also come to the heart of my father's story.

"No," my father answered. "I did not. I might have doubted the truth of Alphonse's tales, but I could hardly doubt the evidence of my own eyes. I was standing beneath the Heartwood Tree, and it would have been sacrilege to take one of its boughs.

I would not have done this, Belle, not even for you."

"Then what happened, Roger?" my mother asked quietly.

"I stepped up close to the tree," my father said, "and placed my palm against the trunk. I'm not quite certain why. To verify by touch that which my eyes were seeing. Or perhaps simply to feel a part of something I had been so certain could not exist. Something so extraordinary."

He looked at my sisters and me, each in turn. "I have seen each of you being born," my father told us. "Held you in my hands within moments of your first breaths, yet still I had never touched anything as alive as the Heartwood Tree felt in that moment.

"I could feel its roots, curling deep into the earth. Feel its sap rising. I could feel new leaves unfurl, petals quiver. And, at the core of it all, it seemed to me that I could feel the very heart of the tree itself, that sweet and bitter combination of love and grief, entwined. Inseparable for as long as the tree should live."

My father paused. "And when I finally dropped my hand," he said, "I felt I saw the world around me with new eyes. For how could one stand in the presence of such strength forged from pain and joy, and not be transformed?"

He gazed into space, as if he could still see the Heartwood Tree in his mind's eye.

"Did you say you had brought in my saddlebags, Dominic?" he asked quietly.

"I did, sir," Dominic answered, his tone slightly mystified. "They are by the door. Shall I bring them to you?"

"If you please," my father replied.

Dominic brought my father's saddlebags to him, placing them on the table, spread out so that the leather strap that passed across the horse's back was in front of Papa and the bags stretched across the width of the table. Then Dominic stepped back, but I noticed he did not return to sit beside April, but stayed close, just behind my father.

Papa rested his hands atop the saddlebags for a moment, as if mustering the courage to reveal what was inside. Then he undid the lacing on one bag and flipped back the flap.

A sweet fragrance wafted out, one that made me think of the whir of bees, of spring birdcalls. My father reached inside the bag and removed a small branch about the same length and width as my forearm. Its bark was dark and ridged, like that of an almond tree. Bursting from the main limb were many fine, short branches, each covered in either red or white blossoms.

My father held the branch in his hands a moment, as if weighing its cost, then reached out and placed it in front of me on the table.

"I did not break a branch from the Heartwood Tree, yet still I have one. But I do not think that it was meant to come to me. I think that it was meant for you, Belle."

Sixteen

"BUT HOW, PAPA? *HOW*?" I CRIED.

I could not quite bring myself to touch the Heartwood branch, for fear it should melt like snow beneath my fingers.

"In just the way Alphonse's tale said it would," my father answered simply. "The tree gave up a branch of its own accord.

"As I stepped away from the trunk, I heard a sharp *crack* overhead and a single limb"—he gestured to the one that now rested on the table in front of me—"*this* limb, came plummeting down. It landed at my feet, directly in front of my boots, in fact. As if anxious to make sure I didn't miss it. I bent down and picked it up."

My father sighed, and I had never seen him look so old.

"There have been moments since," he said, his voice very quiet, "when I have wondered if I might have escaped if I hadn't done this, if I had stepped over the branch of the Heartwood Tree and let it lie where it fell."

"Escape from what?" Dominic asked softly.

My father started, as if he'd forgotten Dominic was standing behind him. "From the Beast," he said. "For that is all I can think to call it."

"The monster," I whispered. "So there *is* a monster in the heart of the Wood."

"There is, indeed," my father said grimly. "And though I still don't understand, its fate is tied to that of the Heartwood. By its own desire, if nothing else."

"What can a Beast desire?" April asked with a shudder.

"Many things, I would imagine," my father said. "But in this case, in the case of the Heartwood Tree, the same as you or I."

"To see the face of true love," I said.

Papa nodded. "No sooner did I pick up the branch of the Heartwood Tree than the Beast was there. It—he—seemed to come from everywhere, and nowhere, all at once. One moment I was bending over to pick up a treasure, the next I was felled by a cry more terrible than anything I have ever heard on this earth. I tumbled to my knees, shielding my face with my hands, no thought of bravery in my mind. That awful cry left no room for it. I was sure I would die."

"'So this is how you repay my kindness!' the creature roared.

'I feed and shelter you, and then you attempt to steal my heart's best hope? Give me one good reason why I shouldn't tear you to pieces right here and now.'

"The cry had been that of a wild animal," my father said. "But the thing before me spoke with a man's voice. At this, my courage broke altogether, for that seemed the most terrible thing of all.

" 'Speak,' the thing before me said. 'Or you will lose the chance to do so.'

" 'I am not a thief,' I said, though I was talking to its feet as I could not bring myself to raise my eyes. 'All my life, I have tried to be a just and honorable man. That has not changed overnight.'

"I felt my heart grow bolder as I spoke, for I knew I spoke the truth. I wasn't about to let some creature of enchantment suggest otherwise, no matter how terrifying it was."

"Good for you, Papa," I murmured.

"I sincerely hope you continue to think so, Belle," my father replied. "I explained how the branch had fallen at my feet and that all I'd done was to pick it up off of the ground.

" 'I have heard the tales about this tree,' I told the Beast. 'Though I never put much stock in them, until now. But if this is truly the Heartwood Tree, then I know it must give of itself freely, or not at all.'

"When I had finished speaking, the Beast was silent for what seemed like a very long time. He made a slow circle around me, his leather boots making no sound as he moved across the grass. Oh, yes. He was clad as a man is," Papa said, to Maman's startled exclamation. "And a rich man, at that, in velvet, leather, and linen. His clothing was more fine than mine. Finally, he came to a halt directly in front of me, precisely where he'd started.

"'Why should the Heartwood choose you?' he demanded. 'It has grown on these lands, my lands, for time out of mind. Why should the tree give you what it has given no one else? You have said that you are honest. Prove it. Speak truth to me now, and do so carefully, for I will know if you lie.'"

My father put a weathered hand over his eyes.

"You told him about me," I said.

"God forgive me," my father answered. "But I did, Belle. I told him of the way you see things in the wood, things that no other eyes nor heart can find."

"Oh, Roger," my mother cried softly.

"No, Maman," I said swiftly as I laid a hand on hers. "Don't. Papa was right to tell the truth."

"I had thought my words might calm the Beast," my father said. "But if anything, they made him more agitated than before. He paced in front of me, his long legs tramping down the grass. Time and again, I tried to raise my eyes. It seemed pitiful that I should kneel on the ground, too terrified to even lift my face when I had done no wrong.

"But try as I might, I could not do it. At last, the Beast stopped pacing and spoke.

"'I will make you a bargain, merchant,' he said. 'For I believe that you have answered my questions honestly and bravely, and that deserves a chance I might not bestow on one who is not as moral as yourself.

"'If you can do what no other living thing has done, if you can look into my face and hold my eyes for the time it takes to count to five, you may take the branch of the Heartwood, leave this place, and never return.'

"'And if I cannot?' I inquired.

"'Then you may go from this place today, but either you or your daughter must return in one week's time. For now that the Heartwood Tree has at last let go of a bough, I must know what it holds inside. Do not think to escape me once you leave the Wood. You have partaken of the magic of this place, and I will know where you go.

"'What say you?' the Beast demanded. 'Will you try?'

"'I will,' I said. For I could see no other way out but to look the creature in the eyes. Here was a chance to free the both of us, Belle."

My father dropped his face into his hands. "I could not do it," he whispered, his voice an agony. "I could not do it, no matter how hard I tried. For every time I lifted my eyes toward his face, a thousand images, each more horrible than the last, seemed to crowd into my mind.

"I told myself that I was being foolish. That I was a man and a man is not afraid to look into an animal's eyes. Outside the

Wood, if a man and beast's eyes meet, it is always the beast who is the first to look away.

"But nothing I told myself made any difference. I could not pass this test, and so I was left to uphold the rest of the bargain.

"'So, merchant,' the Beast said. 'Though you are true and just, I see you are no more brave than other men. Take the Heartwood branch and leave this place, but either you or your daughter must return in one week. I will send for you, so that you do not mistake the time.'

"He began to move away, and so, at last, I stumbled to my feet, only to fall to my knees again and plead for mercy. He must have heard me behind him, for he stopped.

"'I would send your daughter if I were you,' the Beast said. 'Perhaps she will be able to pass the test that you have failed, since she is able to see what no one else does.'

"I did not see him walk any farther," my father said. "With these last words, he was simply gone. I found my way back to my horse and rode for home. The journey seemed to take no time at all, for the road passed quickly out of the Wood and soon I was at my own door."

"And this is where you will remain," my mother said firmly. "Both you and Belle. Or we can set off today, back to the city. We need not go through the Wood. We can go around. Think of it as a bad dream, Roger. But now you are awake; you are back with us."

"I gave my word," my father said.

"In fear of your life, sir," Dominic put in quietly. "Surely you need not honor a bargain made under such terms."

"Perhaps not," said my father. "But—"

"Papa isn't going to go at all," I heard myself say. "I'm the one this Beast really wants. He's made that clear enough. I'm the one who can carve the wood. If not for me, Papa never would have picked up the branch in the first place. I'm the one who should keep the promise."

"How can I allow that?" my father asked, the anguish in his voice ringing as clear as a bell. "What kind of father sends his daughter into danger while he himself stays safe at home?"

"The kind of father who trusts his daughter," I answered. "And who is wise enough to recognize that he has no choice. Surely this Beast only wants what we all do: to see the face of true love. If I can show him that—"

"True love!" my mother suddenly exclaimed. "What can a Beast know of love?"

"Perhaps that is what he wishes to discover," I said.

"Perhaps," cried Maman. "All I hear you say is *if* and *perhaps.* Those are fragile words to pin your hopes on, let alone your life, *ma Belle.*"

I leaned forward then, and did what I'd feared to do, until now. I took the branch of the Heartwood Tree between my hands. The rough bark bit into my palms.

"I have felt . . . different for as long as I can remember," I said quietly. "Even before the space between my name and face

129

became so great that I found a way to disappear inside it."

I lifted up the wood, as if to test its weight, and felt the fine tingling in my hands that always heralded my ability to picture what the wood was holding in its secret heart of hearts.

"I do not know if what I will find inside this wood will be what the Beast wants. But we all know that I'm the only one of us who will find anything at all. I *may* not, but we all know Papa *cannot*. In which case *perhaps* and *if* may be stronger than they sound."

"I do not understand you," my mother said. "It is almost as if you wish to go into danger."

"Of course I don't," I replied. "But I won't send Papa back, not if I can help it."

My father pulled in a breath to speak. I stood up before he could, still cradling the Heartwood bough.

"You are tired, Papa," I said. "All of us are confused and frightened, but none of us need go anywhere right this moment. Let us speak no more of this for now."

I gave Maman a tired smile. "*Perhaps* tomorrow will bring a way out that we cannot see today."

"Perhaps," said my mother. She stood up. "Come upstairs, Roger," she said. "You are tired. A proper rest in your own bed will do you good. Belle is right. Whatever must be decided can wait until at least tomorrow."

Papa and Maman climbed the stairs, their arms around each other. April and Dominic went outside, speaking in quiet voices.

"I'll do the dishes, just this once, mind you," Celeste said. She paused for a moment, gazing at the branch of the Heartwood Tree. "It really is beautiful, isn't it?" she said. "Do you suppose it wants some water?"

"I've been thinking the same thing myself," I said.

And so, while Celeste cleared the dishes, I took the heaviest of our pitchers and filled it with water. I placed the Heartwood branch in the pitcher and carried them both up to my room. I set the pitcher on the windowsill beside my bed. Then I curled up on the bed, gazing at the blossoms of the Heartwood tree, listening to the sound of my parents' voices as they spoke quietly in the next room.

I closed my eyes and felt the small house, which had become our home, safe and snug and comforting, around me. But even with my eyes closed, I saw the petals of the Heartwood Tree, as if their image had been etched onto my eyelids. White as freshly fallen snow; red as heart's blood.

What did the Heartwood hold for the heart of a Beast? I wondered. I fell asleep and dreamed of what my eyes alone might discover.

Seventeen

THE HEARTWOOD BRANCH SAT IN ITS PITCHER ON MY windowsill all week, its petals never fading, its fragrance filling the house. I cannot say my family ever grew comfortable with our strange new situation, but they did become . . . resigned.

There were no more emotional scenes or arguments, though every time I looked at my mother, I saw the fear and sorrow in her eyes. Much as it grieved me to see it, it only strengthened my resolve.

I would not send my father back into the Wood. I must be the one to leave home.

On the morning that Papa or I needed to honor the agreement, I awoke early, even before Celeste, who is always the first one up, to stir up the stove. I washed my hands and face, then stood a moment considering. *What does one wear when going to pay a visit to a Beast?* I wondered. *What else should I bring along?* For I had no idea how long I'd have to stay.

This last thought was all it took to send me hurrying into motion.

Moving quietly, so as not to awaken my sisters, I put on my plainest everyday dress, the one of gray homespun, and laced up my sturdiest pair of shoes. Then I spread my favorite shawl out on the bed and set my bundle of carving tools in the very center, adding an apron and several pairs of stockings to the pile. I folded the ends of the shawl into the middle, and tied it into a bundle I could carry by slipping my arm through the knots.

It wasn't much. But then that was precisely my intention. *That ought to send a message,* I thought. I wasn't coming to impress, and I would stay no longer than I must.

Finally, I lifted the pitcher containing the branch of the Heartwood from off my bedroom windowsill. A scatter of blossoms sifted down. I reached to sweep them up, then decided to let them be. *Let them stay, to welcome me home,* I thought.

I slipped the bundle over my arm and tiptoed from the room. Downstairs in the kitchen, I placed the Heartwood and my belongings on the stool by the back door, went to the stove, stirred up the fire, and put on the kettle. While it was heating up, I opened the back door and looked out. It was as fine a spring morning as anyone could have asked for.

I could see the neat rows of the vegetable garden from where I stood. I had planted carrots, lettuce, beets, peas, pole beans, and tomatoes earlier in the week, trying hard not to wonder whether or not I'd have the opportunity to taste any of the vegetables whose seeds I was so carefully placing in the ground. A faint layer of dew lay on the freshly turned earth. It steamed slightly, where the sun touched it, wisps of ghosts rising up from the ground.

I heard the rattle of the kettle, the signal that the water had begun to boil. I turned toward the stove, but Celeste was already there. She'd come downstairs so quietly I hadn't heard her arrive.

"Thank you for getting things started for me, Belle," Celeste said as she lifted the kettle from the stove and poured the steaming water over the leaves in the teapot.

"I left the real work for you," I said. I stepped back into the kitchen, but left the door open. It was nice to smell the morning air. "All I did was boil water."

"And a fine job you did of it too," Celeste said. "What would you say to pancakes this morning?"

"When have I ever said no to pancakes?" I asked, though, to be honest, I didn't think I could eat a thing. My stomach was full of knots.

Celeste fetched her favorite blue mixing bowl down from the shelf and carried it to the table as if she were preparing to make breakfast as she did on every other morning. But when she went to set down the bowl, it slipped from her hands, gouging the smooth tabletop.

Celeste gave a horrified cry. She rested her hands flat on the table and leaned over them, as if to catch her breath. "I can't do this," she gasped. "I can't act like everything's normal. I just can't. You're really going, aren't you?"

"Yes, I'm really going," I said. I moved to stand beside my sister and laid a consoling hand on her arm. "I have to go. You must see that, Celeste. One of us has to, and I can't let Papa . . ."

My voice faltered, and broke. It was impossible to speak past the enormous weight in my chest, the lump in my throat. All week long, I'd told myself I would be brave. I didn't feel so brave right at that moment.

"Don't," Celeste said. She put her arms around me and held on tight. "Don't you dare cry, Belle. If you start, then I'll start, and we'll wake the whole house. I understand. I think we all do. I just wish there were some other choice."

"I wish that too," I said. "With all my heart. But there isn't one. Unless this Beast, whoever or whatever he is, changes his mind."

"Maybe he will," Celeste said, her tone determined and hopeful. "Or maybe he'll just forget. He said he'd send for you, didn't he? What if—"

She stopped, abruptly, and I felt her arms tighten around my waist. But I was already stepping from the shelter of her arms. For I had heard the same thing she had: the sound of hooves outside.

"Don't look, Belle," Celeste pleaded. "If you don't look, maybe it will go away. We can pretend it isn't there."

"But it *is* there," I said. "And we both know it." I moved to the open door and looked out.

There was a horse standing in the yard beside the vegetable garden. He was the most astonishing color I'd ever seen, a black so deep it was as if the night had changed its form. His mane shimmered blue, like a raven's wing does in bright sunlight.

"I thought princes in fairy tales were supposed to have white horses," Celeste said.

"Ah, but this horse belongs to a Beast and not a prince," I said. "And this is not a fairy tale. It's real life."

"Look," Celeste said. She pointed at the horse's saddle, bit, and bridle. "Silver buckles."

As if he had heard her, the horse tossed his head.

"Silver buckles," I echoed softly. "It seems he doesn't like them any more than I do."

Without warning, Celeste snatched up the Heartwood branch and the shawl with my belongings, and thrust them into my arms.

"Go, Belle," she said. "If you're really determined to do this, then go now, before anyone else comes downstairs. It will only be harder to leave once they do."

I caught my breath. "You're right," I said. "You're absolutely right."

Together, we flew down the back steps and stopped next to

the horse. He took a few prancing steps away, then steadied. I set my belongings on the ground and turned to Celeste.

"Help me up."

Celeste bent and made a cradle with her hands. I put one foot onto them, and she boosted me up. I tossed my leg across the horse's back, riding like a boy. I tucked my skirts in as best I could.

"Say good-bye to them for me," I panted as Celeste handed up my shawl. I set it on the saddle before me, tucking the branch of the Heartwood through the knot. "Tell April not to wait to marry Dominic. And . . . I want to say thank you," I said. "I should have said it long before now."

"Thank you?" my sister asked. "To me? What for?"

"For not telling Paul de la Montaigne I was standing right behind him at that stupid garden party," I said. "For putting my pain before your own. I don't know how I'll ever make it up to you, but I promise you, if I come back, I'll try."

"Don't be ridiculous; of course you'll come back," Celeste replied. "And for the record, Papa was right. Paul de la Montaigne is as dumb as a pailful of earthworms. Forget about him. I certainly have. He was never worth your pain, or mine. Now you'd better get going."

"Tell Papa and Maman I love them," I said.

"I will," Celeste promised, her own voice as breathless as mine. "But I think I've changed my mind. There is something you can do to make up for Paul de la Montaigne."

"What's that?" I asked, even as I felt the horse's muscles bunch beneath my legs.

"Come home."

"I will," I vowed. "I swear to you I will. I'll find whatever it is this Beast wants, then come straight home."

"*I'll* hold you to *that* promise," my sister said.

She stepped back just as the horse reared up, forelegs pawing the air, and uttered one great cry. Then, with a force so hard it made my teeth jar together, his hooves came back down to earth and we galloped from the yard.

"You could consider slowing down," I panted some time later, though it was a miracle I could speak at all. The horse had kept a steady pace, as if afraid to go any slower lest I slip off his back and try to run off on my own.

At the sound of my voice, I saw his ears twitch.

"Our destination isn't going anywhere, is it?" I went on. "I don't expect to make a good impression. I'm already far too windblown for that. And I don't actually imagine your master cares all that much about what I look like anyhow. But it might be nice if I could arrive in one piece. You keep this up, you're going to shake my bones apart."

The horse tossed his head, as if he disapproved of my remarks. But he did slacken his pace, first to a canter and then to a trot. Whether this had to do with my request or the fact that the Wood was up ahead, I could not tell. I brushed my hair back from my face and settled the bundle more firmly in front of me in the saddle.

As we passed beneath the first of the trees, the horse settled into a brisk but easy walk.

"Thank you," I said. "I appreciate your kindness."

He turned his head and lipped the edge of my skirt.

"Oh, so now you want to be friends, do you?" I said with a smile. "After you've gotten your way the whole time."

The horse whickered, a sound like laughter.

"I wonder what you're called," I mused aloud as we continued on. "I hope it's something more imaginative than Midnight. And I wish you could tell me how much farther we have to go."

But here, the horse could provide no answer—none that I could interpret, anyhow. I sat upon his back, my hands resting lightly on the branch of the Heartwood. The trees of the Wood seemed to acknowledge our approach, bending forward as if in stately bows, in a wind they felt but I could not. Dappled sunlight danced across the forest floor.

The horse changed pace again, abandoning his walk for a quick and eager trot. At this, it seemed to me I felt the wind, and more, I heard the sound it made as it brought the treetops together, then pushed them apart, as if they were passing on a message.

Belle is coming. Belle is coming. Belle. Belle. Belle.

Once more the horse shifted pace, into a canter this time. And now I made no request that he hold back, for I thought I understood. He was eager to be home.

"All right," I said. "Go on, boy."

At this, he sprang forward so swiftly that I closed my eyes and held on tight. And so I missed the moment when we passed from the Wood where anyone could travel into the one of enchantment. Whether I would have known the boundary when we crossed it, to this day, I cannot tell.

Finally, with an abruptness that almost tossed me straight over his head, the horse stopped. We'd come to our precipitous halt in front of a pair of elaborately carved wrought-iron gates. In the center of the gate on the right was the silhouette of a man, with one hand outstretched. Opposite him, in the center of the left gate, was a woman, reaching back toward the man.

When the gates were closed, their hands would meet. When the gates were open, they would be apart, yet still reaching for each other. A pair of horses rearing up on their hind legs created a curving arch atop the gates.

"One of those is you, I suppose," I said. The horse gave his head a toss. As if at the sound of my voice, the gates swung open. Just as my father had said, they did not make a sound.

I gasped. Perhaps it was just the shadow of a nearby tree, but as the gate opened, the figure of the man altered, if only for a moment. Instead of the smooth lines that suggested a nobleman in fine clothes, it seemed the silhouette grew jagged; desperation etched in every line. It looked like a soul in torment.

But with the gate swung wide, the shadow passed, and I was gazing once again at a young man reaching toward his sweetheart.

"I guess this means we can go in," I said. The horse tossed

his head and stamped, setting the silver buckles on his harness jangling. But he stayed right where he was. And all of a sudden, I understood.

This Beast doesn't miss a trick, does he? I thought.

"May I please come in?" I called out, my voice clear and strong. I'd been a little concerned about that, if the truth must be told. Talking to the horse was one thing, to his master, quite another. At any rate, there could be no harm in being polite. Less chance of being eaten on the spot, or so I sincerely hoped.

"My name is Annabelle Evangeline Delaurier," I went on. "I have come to honor my father's debt, to return the branch of the Heartwood Tree. I have come of my own accord. I would like to enter, if you'll let me."

The horse whickered its approval. There was a beat of silence. Then, as if he'd heard an answer that I couldn't, the horse walked through the gates.

Don't look back, Belle, I thought. *Don't watch those gates shut fast behind you.*

But of course I did it anyhow. I turned and watched the gates that marked the place between the world I thought I understood and one I was quite certain I did not, close silently behind me. The man's and the woman's outstretched hands were truly clasped together now. The young couple was reunited.

I turned my face away. Toward the heart of the Wood. The home of the Beast, the monster.

Eighteen

THE REMAINDER OF MY JOURNEY WAS JUST AS MY FATHER had described. The path the horse and I trod was narrow, and made of ivory-colored stones so cunningly made there was not a chink for a single blade of grass to grow. On one side, an orchard of fruit trees stretched into the distance. On the other, roses grew in great profusion, tumbling over one another in what must have once been a series of formal flower beds, long gone wild. The scent of the flowers was so strong I could almost see it in the air. And, woven in so tightly it could not be separated out, was also the bitter tang of loneliness.

The path wound for about half a mile, then broadened out.

The horse rounded a gentle curve, and suddenly, I could see the rise with the great stone house and its courtyard and stable sprawling across the top. The horse moved steadily up the hill until he reached the courtyard, then stopped. The house was to my left now, and the stables to the right. I looked around, but could see nowhere I could easily dismount. So I sat on the horse's back, my palms against the bark of the Heartwood Tree, as if for good luck, and waited.

It's your move, Beast, I thought.

I'd like to be able to say that my first sight of him was magical and supernatural, that he appeared from out of nowhere with a crash of thunder and a puff of smoke. Papa had said the Beast had seemed to come from out of thin air, from everywhere and nowhere, all at once. So expecting the extraordinary hardly seemed far-fetched.

In my case, he came from the stables, as if he were a stable boy preparing the stall for the horse. It was so prosaic, I might have laughed, but even I am not that brave. It's hard to laugh when your heart is in your throat.

Though I suppose it could be said that he did appear magically. For, one moment, the horse and I were alone in the courtyard. And, in the next, there was a figure, a shadow within a shadow, standing in the open stable door.

I gave a jolt, and the horse beneath me shifted a step, steadied, then pawed the ground with one dark hoof, as if annoyed at my response.

"I'm sorry," I whispered. "But this isn't exactly easy for me, you know."

The horse blew out a breath, and the figure in the doorway stepped forward into the light. I shivered, even as the air in the courtyard seemed to ripple with heat. My heart began to beat in hard, fast strokes, so loudly it would have been a miracle if he didn't hear it all the way across the courtyard.

He was tall.

That was my first thought. Even from a distance, and from my vantage point on the back of a high horse, he was tall. Lean and rangy like a wolf, was my second, not particularly comforting, thought. I felt my courage start to waver.

You can do this. You have to do this, Belle, I thought.

Half a dozen steps the Beast strode toward me, the soles of his boots making not a single sound. Then he stopped. I had no idea why. The horse stretched his neck, as if testing the bit between his teeth.

"I suppose," I heard a deep voice say. "That you are quite real."

I gasped, for I felt his voice pass through my skin, through muscle and flesh, until it came to rest in the marrow of my bones. Papa had said the Beast had the voice of a man, but this was not quite accurate, I thought.

For no human being I had ever met spoke in a voice like that, sounding heart and mind together, at once, as one. A Beast may have the ability to camouflage its skin. Men are better at hiding their hearts.

"I don't understand you," I somehow found a way to reply. "I am Belle Delaurier," I said, as I had at the gate. "I am here by your order. You gave my father shelter, and he took away a gift you did not wish to bestow. I have come to bring it back and to fulfill his promise."

The Beast took three more steps. Two more, and he would be close enough to touch.

"So you *are* real," he murmured, almost as if speaking to himself. "I have not imagined you. You are real. You have come. I see a dark gray dress on my horse's back, strong hands on the reins, and your hair . . ."

He paused, and I had the sense he was studying me intently. "Your hair curls and it is brown. But your face . . ." His voice faltered and broke off. "Your face eludes me," he continued after a moment. "Your features slip in and out of focus, like a star at the end of a telescope."

"I am not a star," I said, a sudden ache in my throat. "I'm just a girl named Annabelle."

"Annabelle," he echoed, and I seemed to feel the strange power of his voice in every part of me. As if it were seeking the way to make me visible. "But I thought that you said . . . Belle?"

"Belle is my nickname," I answered. "It's what I've always been called. I think that may be your problem—with my face, I mean. It makes you think you're supposed to look for Beauty."

"And I can't find what isn't there?" the Beast said. "Is that your point?"

"It is," I replied.

He took one more step, and then another until he was standing right beside me.

"Real and honest," he said. "A powerful combination. You do not spare feelings, not even your own. So I will tell you a truth of my own in exchange for yours: What I can and cannot see is not determined by your face, alone, Belle Delaurier. It is . . . part of the reason I reside in this place, so that I might learn to use my eyes."

"I don't understand," I said once more.

"You will," he answered. "Or so I hope, in time."

He placed a hand against the horse's flank then, not an inch from my knee. I stared down. Like the rest of him, his hand was long and lean, though broad across the knuckles.

A strong and capable hand, I thought. One that could both cradle and crush. It was covered in a fine layer of fur, copper-colored, like the coat of a fox. The tapering fingers ended in short nails, pointed at the tips. They looked sharp.

The horse turned his head and rubbed it along the Beast's arm. The Beast lifted that hand and stroked it along the horse's nose.

"What is your horse called?" I blurted out.

The hand stilled for an instant, then continued its motion. "Corbeau."

"Raven," I said. The horse tossed its head, as if acknowledging its name. "It suits him, and it's a much better name than Midnight."

146

The Beast made a sudden sound, like a strange, harsh bark. I started, and the horse shied. The Beast stepped back.

"I'm sorry," I said, when Corbeau was calm once more. I stroked a hand along the horse's neck, on the opposite side from where the Beast stood. He made no move to step in close again, I noticed. "I'm sorry. I didn't mean to do that."

"I know you didn't," the Beast said. "I think that's the problem. For the record, I don't intend to eat you. I don't intend you any harm."

"What do you want, then?" I asked.

"Company, for one thing," the Beast replied. He made a gesture in my direction, and I managed to keep myself still this time. "And to see what the Heartwood holds. Your father said you might be able to show me this."

"I hope so."

"Will it take long?"

I hope not, I thought. *For both our sakes.*

"That is up to the wood itself, not to me," I answered honestly. "Every piece of wood I've ever touched has shown me its secret eventually. Some take longer to reveal what they hold on the inside than others. The Heartwood has held on to its secrets for a very long time."

"That is so," the Beast concurred. There was a quick pause. "Thank you, Annabelle."

"What for?" I asked. "I haven't done anything yet."

"Oh, but you have," he countered. "You came, and you have

spoken the truth twice now, even though it frightens you to do so. Another person might have given me an easier answer, one they imagined I might like to hear. You did not."

He stepped to stand beside the horse once more. "I'm sure you'd rather be a million miles away, but I am glad that you have come, Annabelle."

"If you will call me that," I answered, "then I will try to be glad I'm here as well." For, in only a few minutes with this stranger, this Beast had done what I had been unable to convince my family to do in nearly ten years: He had called me Annabelle.

"And I will do my best to see, and to reveal, what the Heartwood holds," I went on. "Though, since we're busy appreciating the honesty, I should probably mention that I can't promise that what I find will be what you want. My ability is to see truly, not on command."

"If you see truly, then what you reveal will *be* what I want," the Beast replied. "And now, I don't suppose I could persuade you to come down off Corbeau. I'm sure he's ready for his stall."

"Of course," I said, though my lips felt stiff. It was clear he meant to help me down himself.

I handed down the bundle of my shawl, being careful not to touch him. He took it from me just as carefully, then set it beside him on the cobblestones. I settled the branch of the Heartwood in the nook of one elbow, as if it were an infant.

"Hand it to me," the Beast said simply. "I'll give it back when you're on the ground."

For the space of time it took for me to draw a breath, I was certain that I was going to say no. But, at the last instant, I changed my mind. Cradling the branch between my palms, one on either end, I leaned down. The Beast reached out and grasped the Heartwood in the middle. A tingle, so sharp it was almost pain, shot into my hands and up my arms. I think I made a sound.

The Beast froze, his great hands gripping the Heartwood so tightly that I saw his knuckles beneath the copper-colored fur, for they had turned stark white.

"Look at me, Annabelle," he demanded in that fierce, compelling voice. "Look into my face, into my eyes for the span of time it takes to count to five. Look at me and let me see you. Look at me and free us both."

The tingling in my arms was truly pain now. Spreading across my shoulders, burrowing into my chest, aiming straight for my heart. When it reached it, I would be transformed. Whether it would be as simple as dying, I could not tell. But of one thing I was certain: I would no longer be the Belle Delaurier I knew.

And it was because of him, this strange combination of man and beast that stood before me.

"No," I said. "I can't. I'm sorry."

He made a dark sound, deep within his chest, and I understood that my own pain was nothing.

"Then let go of the Heartwood," he commanded.

I set my teeth. "I'm trying."

It was Corbeau who broke the deadlock, turning his head without warning to sink his teeth deep into the Beast's shoulder. The Beast gave a startled exclamation, released the Heartwood, and stepped back. The second we were no longer touching the wood together, my fingers loosened of their own accord. I released the branch and it fell, landing on the bundle of my belongings.

I cradled my hands in my lap, one curved inside the other. My fingers were stiff and painful. I flexed them, rubbing them as if to bring back the circulation after too long out in the cold. Without a word, the Beast bent to retrieve my bundle and the branch of the Heartwood.

"I can get down myself," I hurried into speech, throwing one leg over Corbeau's neck as I did so. I slid along his flank to the ground, the impact of the cobblestones jarring every bone in my body. I leaned against the horse for a moment, waiting for my legs to steady. "And I can stable Corbeau as well, if you'll let me. I'd like to."

"As you wish," the Beast said, turning away. I turned to the horse.

"All right," I whispered against his neck. "It's going to be all right. Come along now, Corbeau."

The horse followed me obediently, as if I were the one who cared for him every night. Just as we reached the door of the stable, the Beast spoke once more.

"Why did you think the horse would be called Midnight?" he asked. "And why were you pleased when he was not?"

I paused, one hand on Corbeau's neck, though I did not turn back. "Because of his color," I answered. "And because it seemed too obvious a choice."

Again, he made that sound in his throat that had so startled me before. *He's laughing,* I realized.

"I think you'll find not much around here makes the obvious choice. Thank you for caring for my horse, Annabelle."

"You're welcome," I said.

"I'll wait for you inside."

If you're trying to make me hurry, that's not the way to do it, I thought.

I did turn back then, to ask how in the world I would find him inside that great stone house, and discovered he'd pulled the trick I'd expected earlier.

He'd vanished into thin air, for he was nowhere in sight.

Nineteen

I STABLED CORBEAU, TAKING OFF THE SADDLE AND HAR-
ness, finding the place to stow them where they belonged, then
caring for him as carefully as if he were my own horse. I brushed
him so long and well I could almost see myself reflected in his
glossy dark coat, and he, himself, was stamping in impatience,
eager for the meal that was still to come.

At long last, more reluctantly than I liked to admit, I put
the brush and currycomb away and fed Corbeau. I stayed beside
him, leaning my head against his smooth, warm flank, listening
to his strong teeth make fast work of his evening meal of oats.

"You like him, don't you?" I murmured. "And he likes
you." The stable was as immaculate as Corbeau himself.

"That's good news, isn't it? That he's capable of affection?"

Because you're hoping what, precisely, Belle? I thought. *That he'll like you, too? Be satisfied with not being eaten and be done with it.*

Corbeau blew out a great snuffling breath, as clear a request to be left in peace as if he'd spoken. Which, come to think of it, I suppose he had.

"All right," I said. "I'm stalling. I admit it. There's no need to get all huffy."

Corbeau turned his head then, regarding me with one dark eye. "I'm going to go inside the house now," I said. "I am, honestly. Just as soon as I remember how to breathe."

For, abruptly, I felt dizzy and light-headed. My heart pounded, as if I'd been running.

I stamped my foot in frustration, and Corbeau showed his teeth. "This is ridiculous," I said. "And it's going to stop right now. What was the use of coming this far if I won't go any farther? I'm going inside that house. I'm going right now."

On impulse, I leaned over and gave Corbeau's neck a kiss. Then I turned and walked from the stable, wishing I didn't feel like I was leaving behind my one and only friend.

The doors to the great stone house were shut, and though I did not give myself permission to take this as a sign to turn around and run in the opposite direction, I did put off going inside for one moment more. For the doors gave me a surprise. They were made of wood and elaborately carved. And, like the gates I'd passed through to enter the Beast's domain, they showed a man and woman, reaching toward each other.

It was easy to see that the couple was nobly born. For the carving was so intricate and detailed I could see the lace the man wore at collar and cuffs, and the long string of pearls the woman wore at her throat.

Who are you? I wondered.

Once again, with the doors shut fast, the couple's hands were joined. I hesitated a moment longer, reluctant to break that clasp, for it seemed to me that these were two who should never be parted for long.

Nor will they be, I chastised myself. *Only for the amount of time it takes the doors to open and close. Stop putting off going inside, Belle. You can't stand on the front step forever.*

I sighed. Then I walked up the last two steps, setting my hands against the place where the couple's hands met. That was all it took to get the doors to open. As the gates had, the great wooden doors of the house swept back silently. The arms of the figures on the doors swung wide, in a gesture that looked like a grand welcome.

I stepped across the threshold.

The entry hall was a dazzle of colors as the light streamed in from stained glass windows high above. It both obscured and illuminated the images on the tiles beneath my feet. For, just as

Papa had described, the entry hall of the house was covered in a mosaic, many parts working together to form a whole.

Everything here tells a story, I realized. Whether it was the same one, over and over again, or some fresh tale each and every time, I couldn't yet tell. *Perhaps with enough time,* I thought, then caught myself short.

I was here to discover what lay hidden within the Heartwood branch. That, and nothing more. The sooner I did so, the sooner I could keep my promise to Celeste, and to myself: the sooner I could return home. I had no business getting sidetracked by whatever stories might lie hidden in this place, no matter how artfully told.

"There you are," I heard the Beast say, interrupting my thoughts. He materialized at the back of the entry hall, perhaps from the study where my father had sheltered. He strode forward into the light until we were both illuminated by the colors streaming down from the windows above. I, in a pool of yellow; he, in a patch just a shade lighter than indigo. I looked up and saw that the color came from the sunlight passing through the image of a woman dressed in a dark blue gown.

Look how he manages to find the shadows even when the sun is shining on him, I thought.

"I wondered if perhaps you meant to stay in the stables with Corbeau," the Beast went on.

So there was to be no reference to the strange and uncomfortable moment in the courtyard, when he had all but begged me to look into his face, to gaze into his eyes. That was perfectly fine with me.

"I considered it," I answered lightly. I did my best to seem as if I was really looking at him, casting a quick glance upward in the general vicinity of his face, before letting my gaze settle on a place slightly over his left shoulder, at about the height of his earlobe—if I'd actually been able to find his earlobe beneath all that hair. For now, as I did my best *not* to look at him, I seemed to see a hundred things that I had not before.

He had a man's hair upon his head, just a shade darker than the copper fur that covered the backs of his hands. It curled in wild profusion, long enough to brush down to his impossibly broad shoulders. It was almost as if the very form of him could not quite make up its mind. Was he a man, or was he a beast? I wondered, abruptly and uncomfortably, whether this might be the true definition of a monster: a being that was neither one thing nor another.

"Let me show you to your room," the Beast—for by now I was incapable of thinking of him by any other name—said, precisely as if he were an innkeeper and I, a guest to be welcomed and made comfortable. "Perhaps that will make you feel better about coming indoors."

And perhaps I'll learn to sing like a nightingale, I thought, though I chose not to mention that possibility aloud.

I nodded to show that I would follow his lead. We proceeded up a broad set of central stairs, side by side. They were made of the same gray stone as the rest of the house, but running down the center was a wide runner of bright blue.

"I feel as if I'm walking up a waterfall," I said.

He made what I sincerely hoped was an appreciative grunt. *And walking next to you is like hiking up one mountain with another at your side,* I thought.

I had seen that he was tall. It was the first thing that I'd noticed. But it was one thing to *see* it, looking down from the back of a large horse, and another thing to *feel* it, walking with him. My head reached no higher than the center of his chest.

Just high enough to peer into his heart, I thought. Then wished I hadn't, for I wasn't all that sure I wanted to discover what a Beast's heart might hold.

The stairs ended in a broad landing with three halls heading off in different directions. One straight ahead, and one each to the left and right.

"I have put you this direction," the Beast said, indicating that we would proceed along the passage to the right. "On this side of the house, the windows overlook the lake."

And the Heartwood Tree, I thought.

"Where are your rooms?" I asked, then did my best not to wince, for it sounded as if I was trying to find out how far apart our rooms were without asking the question directly.

"All around you," the Beast answered shortly. "For everything here is mine. But if you're asking where I sleep, I have no fixed place. Sometimes I stay indoors at night. More often I do not."

So you are nocturnal, like an animal, I thought.

"Don't you have a favorite room?" I asked, determined to find a safe topic.

"I do," the Beast replied, after a brief pause. "The study. Where your father spent the night."

"You are fond of books, then," I persevered.

"I am," he said. "Though I am also rather hard on them." The Beast made a strange gesture, clicking his long, sharp nails together. "This is your room."

The Beast stopped before a closed door, turned the knob, and pushed the door open wide. Before me stretched an endless carpet of fresh spring green, precisely the same color as a new lawn. To the left, a great canopy bed swathed in pale peach silk rested on a dais of white marble. On the right was a great wooden wardrobe. But it was what I saw straight ahead that captured my attention and held it.

For the back wall of the room was not a wall at all. Instead, it was a series of windows so clear I would not have known they were there save for the frames that held the panes in place. Through them I could see the sparkle of the lake, the movement of the clouds as they scudded across the clear blue sky. I was across the threshold and moving toward the windows almost before I realized what I'd done.

"You like it, then," the Beast said.

"Of course I like it," I responded. I could see that there was a wide balcony bordered by a stone balustrade outside the windows. In the center was a little table with just one chair pulled up before it. Hidden by the bulk of the wardrobe was the door that would take me to the outside. It was made of mahogany, polished until it gleamed ruby red. In its center was a crystal doorknob.

"It's beautiful," I said. "Everything about it is beautiful. Do the windows open?"

"Place your hand upon whichever pane of glass you choose and it will yield before your touch," the Beast said. "When you wish it to return, call it back."

I stopped short, astonished, then continued the rest of the distance to the windows more slowly. I lifted one hand, then pressed my palm against the closest pane of glass. I felt a sharp cold, as if I'd plunged my fingers into ice, and then, with a sound I thought might be laughter, the glass seemed to whisk away and my hand moved through into the open air.

I snatched my hand back, considered it a moment, then extended it again. This time my hand passed straight through. The glass was simply . . . not there. I wiggled my fingers experimentally, then brought them indoors once more.

"Thank you very much for the demonstration. Now come back, please," I said.

I heard a sigh, as if someone had exhaled a breath into the room, and saw that the pane of glass was back in place.

"Stay put now, if you please," I said, and set my fingertips against it. The glass did as I instructed. It was precisely as the

Beast had said. If I willed the pane of glass to open, it would do so. Otherwise, it was simply a pane of glass.

"I thought you might be joking," I said as I turned back toward the Beast.

"Why would I do that?" he asked. "How much humor do you think a beast has?"

"I imagine that depends on the beast," I said. I frowned, for I realized suddenly that he was still standing in the hall. "Why are you out there?"

He shifted his weight, as if uncomfortable.

"This is *your* room," he said. "No one may enter except by your permission."

"Not even you?"

"Not even me."

Slowly, I moved back across the floor until we faced each other across the threshold, just a little too close for comfort.

"You deny yourself a place in your own home? Why would you do that?"

"Because I wanted you to have a place here you could call your own, a place you could feel safe."

"Am I in some danger, then?"

"From me, no," the Beast said. "But from your own fears of me and your surroundings, I think the answer may be yes."

He shifted his weight again. "I would like—" He stopped, then tried again. "Please do not misunderstand me," he said. "You have done an impressive job this morning, Annabelle.

You've been polite, but you've shown also that you have back-bone. Both of which are very nice, but they do not alter the heart of the matter.

"You did not come here of your own free will."

"There's an easy way out of that," I answered. "Let me go."

"No," he said without hesitation. "Not yet. Not until you can show me what the Heartwood holds."

"So until then, no matter how lovely and magical it is, this place is still a prison."

Now it was the Beast who took a step forward, until the tips of his boots nudged right up against the doorway. "It has always been a prison," he said. "A very beautiful one, that much is true, but a prison nevertheless. I find it helps if you don't try quite so hard *not* to see the bars."

He took a single step back. "Within the boundaries of this place you may go anywhere you like," he went on. "But you may not go beyond them. The same applies to me, if it makes you feel any better."

"Thank you for telling me," I said. "But it doesn't."

"I didn't think it would," he replied.

He picked up my shawl and the branch of the Heartwood, both of which had been sitting beside the door in the hall. "Here are your belongings. Your time is yours to spend as you wish, though I'd like to make a request."

It's your house, I thought. *You can do whatever you like.*

"I'm listening," I said. Not the most gracious response, but standing there I realized suddenly how very tired I was. Just getting here had taken all my strength, and now he wanted one thing more.

"Please," I said, when he still remained silent. "Go on."

"I'm hoping you will consent to join me each day, just at twilight," the Beast replied. "I have become reconciled to many things, but not to being utterly alone as day gives way to night. If you will give me your company, I think it would make the moment easier to bear."

"How will I know where to find you?" I asked.

"I'll find you," the Beast said. "If you consent."

"I consent, just don't . . ." I sighed. There was no way forward but to sound ridiculous or to give offense, or both. "I would appreciate it if you wouldn't sneak up on me," I said. "Your sudden appearances and disappearances can be a little alarming."

"That is fair enough," the Beast said. "I will do my best not to alarm you. Until tonight then, Annabelle."

Without another word, he turned and strode away. I closed the door quietly behind him. Then, carrying the Heartwood branch, I walked back across the room, opened the door to the balcony, and stepped out. The air was clean and brisk, and I inhaled deeply. I sat down at the table, and though the view beyond my balcony was compelling, all my attention was cradled within my palms.

I closed my eyes, waiting for the tingle that would be the

signal that soon I'd know what the wood held within it, the image it carried in its heart of hearts. But, though I sat all that afternoon, sat until the air grew chill and the sun began to sink in the sky, I felt no stirring of my Gift.

I felt nothing, nothing at all.

And finally, for the first time, I felt truly afraid. Afraid for my own life. Not that the Beast would harm me, but that my existence might come to be as his was. That the loneliness of this place, no matter how beautiful it was, would soon become his and mine combined.

I gripped the Heartwood tightly in my hands, the deeply grooved bark biting into my palms.

Help me, I thought. *Help me to see truly. Help me find the secret of your heart.*

Help me to find the way to free the Beast, and myself.

Twenty

OUR DAYS SOON FELL INTO A SOMEWHAT COMFORTABLE routine. The Beast and I kept out of each other's way as much as possible during the day, but, no matter where in the house or on the grounds I was, he always found me, just at twilight. Sometimes we would sit in the study, while he pointed out his favorite books. But more often, as the weather was warm, we stayed outdoors. Soon, I had been all over the grounds that were within easy walking distance of the great stone house.

I was beginning to learn my way around in other ways, as well. In addition to the panes of glass in my windows, there were doors that would open merely with a wish, set side by side with ones I could not open at all. I had only to think of a food I wanted to eat and it would appear, sometimes literally, before me. The first time this happened I was caught completely unawares and put my foot down squarely in a fresh strawberry pie. I soon learned to be stationary (and preferably seated) when I thought of food.

I tried very hard not to think too much of home. For when I did this, the house felt most like a prison, albeit a lovely and magical one.

But I did not let my explorations distract me from my purpose. Every day, I took the Heartwood into my hands, trying to listen as it whispered its secrets, straining to see into its heart of hearts. I stood beneath the tree itself for hours on end, gazing up into its boughs. I laid my hands against the trunk, as Papa had. I even kicked off my shoes and climbed into the branches, the bark snagging holes in my stockings.

But no matter what I did, the Heartwood remained silent. The secrets it carried, it kept to itself. And every evening, just at nightfall, the Beast repeated the request he'd made the day I first arrived. That I look into his face and gaze into his eyes for the time it took to count to five. Each and every night I gave the same reply.

"No. I can't. I'm sorry."

Until, at last, I began to grow tired of the struggle. Of all the things I couldn't do. And I wondered how much longer we could go on as we were.

"Why five?" I asked one night. The Beast and I were sitting

together in the pergola, by the shores of the lake. He had not made his daily request yet, but I could tell it was coming. The sun had just begun to sink, plunging into the waters of the lake like a gold coin tossed to make a wish.

"What?" the Beast asked, as if his mind had been far away, drifting on the waters of the lake, perhaps, as his body sat, huge and solid, at my side.

"You always ask the same thing," I said. "You always ask me to look at you for the time it takes to count to five. Why that number? Does it mean something, or did you just choose it at random?"

"I didn't choose it at all," the Beast replied. If he was surprised that I'd brought up the matter of his request myself, he did not show it. But then, I didn't have any of the usual landmarks to go by. It's hard to learn to know someone when you can't see their face or look into their eyes.

What a curious couple we are, I thought, then sat up a little straighter, as if poked by a pin. *You're not a couple at all, Belle,* I reminded myself.

"Then why?" I inquired. "If you didn't choose the number, who did?"

He turned his head then, as if he wished he could read my expression. "Why do you want to know?"

I felt a burst of emotion, frustration and impatience combined. At least I was making an effort to understand. All he did was ask the same question every single night.

Though we were often together as the sun went down, I had always stayed alone in my own room after dark. This had been my own decision, and it had seemed a prudent choice. Even in the world I knew, it was not always safe to be out after dark. And there was so very much about this place I did not know.

"There is nothing in the dark that will deliberately seek you out to harm you, nothing present in the dark that does not dwell in the light, as well," the Beast replied. "But the dark provides a kind of freedom. It is a time when some things here become more of what they truly are."

"And what is that?" I asked.

"Wild."

I let this sink in, weighing the options, for I had the very strong feeling he was including himself.

"Thank you for the warning," I said. "But I believe I would still like to go. I can go on my own, if you don't wish to take me. I know how to row a boat."

But the Beast was already shaking his head. "No. If going out on the lake is what you wish, then it will be my pleasure to take you."

"That is what I wish."

"Then let us go."

Much to my astonishment, he offered an arm, precisely as if we were a young lady and gentleman out for an evening's stroll. I hesitated. Aside from that first day, when he'd tried to lift me from the horse, we had been very careful not to touch each other. And he had not gone near the Heartwood branch again. It was always safe in my room, or on the balcony outside.

I steadied my hand, then tucked my fingers lightly into the crook of his arm. A shudder passed through him, of pain or pleasure I could not tell.

The Beast wore velvet. He almost always did, and the fabric was rich and smooth beneath my fingertips. And for once I was dressed as finely as he, for I had at long last given up the simple dress I'd brought with me in favor of one from the wardrobe. I'd put off doing this for as long as possible. Wearing the clothes the Beast provided felt too much like settling in. But I had brought only one dress, and I couldn't wear it every day forever.

The one I'd finally decided on was a deep blue with a full skirt, and a lace undershift that showed at the bodice and cuffs. It wasn't until I was halfway down the stairs that I realized why I'd chosen it over all the others: The dress was the same shade as the gown worn by the woman in the stained glass window, the window that had hid the Beast in shadow that first afternoon. Like the Beast's own clothing, it was velvet. I felt its luxurious weight with every step I took, a far cry from my usual homespun.

"Who is the young couple?" I asked. "The one on the gate, and on the front door?"

"You are full of questions tonight," the Beast observed. Not quite the response I was hoping for. We reached the pier and proceeded down it toward the boat, our shoes making hollow sounds against the wood.

"I'm always full of questions," I admitted with a sigh. "It used to drive my mother crazy when I was a child. I'd try my best not to ask them, but it would always make things worse. I'd store them up only to let them loose in a great flood, just like tonight. I therefore solemnly promise not to ask any more questions this evening."

"You will have a hard time keeping that promise, I think," he remarked.

I laughed before I could catch myself. "And I think that sounds just like a clever challenge."

We reached the end of the pier. I released his arm, and watched as the Beast stepped down into the rowboat. It rocked beneath his weight then steadied.

"How about this?" I said, on impulse. "Let's see which one of us can go the longest without asking a question." I heard him pull in a breath. "And the one I asked just now doesn't count," I hurried on. "Whoever gives in and asks first must receive a truthful answer, but then the other gets to ask two questions, and receive two truthful answers in return."

He gave a grunt. "You have brothers and sisters, don't you?"

"Two sisters," I said. "Stop trying to weasel out. Is it settled?"

"I don't suppose that counts either," the Beast said.

"Of course not. We're still establishing the rules. And don't think I didn't notice the way you snuck in a question. Rhetorical questions are considered cheating, by the way."

"You drive a hard bargain," he observed.

So do you, I thought. But I was determined not to stray into potentially unpleasant territory.

"Very well. I will play this questions game," the Beast said. "Now hold still."

I opened my mouth to ask the obvious question, then closed it again. "Very sneaky," I replied. "I am standing still. I eagerly await your explanation as to why."

"So I can lift you down into the boat, of course," he said. Perhaps I was becoming accustomed to the timbre and cadence of his voice, but I could *hear* the smile within it. He was enjoying himself.

"I can get down myself," I protested.

"No," he countered at once. "It's too far for you to step, as I did, and it's not safe for you to jump. If you want to go out on the lake, you have to let me help you down. That's *my* bargain, Belle."

Don't call me that, I almost snapped. Instead I bit down, hard, on the tip of my tongue.

"I'm standing still," I said.

He reached out, grasped me tightly around the waist, and lifted me up. His hands were so large they almost spanned my waist. My stomach made a strange little lurch. I put my hands on his shoulders to steady myself.

He is so strong, I thought. Strong enough to snap me in two without breaking a sweat. Strong enough to shelter me from whatever harm might come. I felt my arms begin to tremble, suddenly, as if it were I who carried some extra weight. The wind whisked by to snatch at my skirts, billowing them into a great cloud of dark blue fabric. I felt like I was flying.

The Beast lifted me up, high above his head. I threw my own head back and laughed at the unexpected glory of it. The stars were just beginning to spangle in the sky overhead. From the unseen far shore of the lake, I heard a night bird call.

The Beast made a half turn, the boat rocking a little under his feet. I put my arms around his neck and held on tighter.

He stopped, the boat steadied, and he set me down, sliding me along the length of his body. Just for a moment, my face brushed against his. I heard him pull in a sudden breath even as I made a sound of wonder. For there was something unexpected here, a thing my senses were trying to tell me but my mind refused to grasp. Then my feet were in the boat. He took a half step back, grasping my forearms to keep me steady as the boat rocked once again. As soon as the motion stopped, he let me go.

Heart roaring in my ears, I sank down onto the wooden seat in the bow. Without a word, the Beast took his place in the stern and unshipped the oars. Then he cast off, using the end of one oar to push us away from the pier. He rowed steadily and quietly for several minutes. I sat, and waited for my heart to steady, watching the stars come out.

"It's very beautiful," I said finally.

"Indeed, it is. It will be even more lovely when the moon is up." He continued to row, the motion smooth and steady. "You asked me a question earlier."

"I asked several questions earlier."

"True enough. This one was of a . . . numeric nature. You wanted to know why I ask you to look into my eyes for the space of time it takes to count to five."

"Only if you feel like telling me," I said quickly.

"It's not so very complicated," the Beast replied. "Five for five heartbeats, the length of time it takes to breathe in or out. For that is how quickly a life may change, for better or for ill. The time it takes to make up, or change, your mind."

"That's it?" I cried. "No story of enchantment, of brother against brother or son against father?"

Then I dropped my head down into my hands when I realized what I'd done.

"There is some of that, as well," the Beast said mildly. "But that tale has not been spoken in many years, and then only in daylight. It is . . . not a tale for the dark." There was a pause, during which he began to row once more. "I believe you owe me several answers, Annabelle."

"Yes, yes," I said. "All right. I know." I lifted my head, straightened my shoulders, and lifted my chin. "I'm ready."

"You might," he observed in a mild voice, "try to sound a little less as if you were about to face a firing squad. You said you came here of your own free will. Did you mean it?"

"Within reason," I replied. "One of us had to come, either Papa or I. I couldn't let it be Papa. Losing him would devastate my mother, I think, but more than that . . ."

I broke off.

"More than that?" the Beast prompted.

"You want to know what lies within the Heartwood," I said. "To see the face of true love. Papa cannot show you that. Only I can."

"Then why haven't you?" he asked, his voice very, very quiet.

"I honestly don't know. It's never been this difficult before. Usually, all I have to do is hold a piece of wood in my hands to see what it holds inside it.

"But with the Heartwood, it's almost as if I'm not looking in the right place, as if there's some extra angle I'm supposed to consider, some additional question I'm supposed to ask.

"I'd like to find the answer just as much as you want me to," I said. "It's the only way I can go home."

The wood of the oars scraped softly against their metal locks as the Beast slid the oars forward, then pulled back, slowly.

"You find it so unpleasant here, then?" he asked.

I shook my head. "No. It isn't that. It's very beautiful here, and I think that you . . ." I paused for a moment, to be certain of what I wanted to say. "You are doing your best to take my mind off the fact that I can't go home. You have been very kind. But this isn't my home. You must see that."

"I see it very well."

"What do you see when you look at me?" I suddenly asked.

The Beast lifted his head. I could feel his eyes on me in the gathering dark. *Just do it, Belle,* I thought. *Look up. How hard can it be to look into his eyes?*

But in spite of my mind's questioning, my eyes would not obey. It was like the Heartwood, only worse. For I wasn't altogether certain I wanted to discover the secrets of the Beast's face.

"Bits and pieces," the Beast said at last. "Tonight, for instance, I can see that you have on a blue velvet dress. I already know that your hair is brown and that it curls, and that the top of your head reaches no higher than the center of my chest.

"But your face defeats me utterly. I cannot see your features, the shape of your lips, the color of your eyes. Although I think . . ." He broke off and leaned forward as if to examine something. "That you have a dimple in your chin."

"I do," I acknowledged, not quite sure how I felt that he'd discovered this. He'd seen me more clearly than anyone had in years. "My eyes are—" I began.

"No!" he interrupted swiftly. "Don't tell me. It's important I discover this for myself, with my own eyes."

There was a charged silence. *Here it comes,* I thought.

"Please don't ask me," I said. "Just this once. Just for tonight."

He leaned back then, and I could almost hear the effort that it cost him to do as I asked.

"Look into the water, Annabelle," he said at last. "You can see the stars."

So grateful I thought I might weep, I turned, rested my hands on the gunwale, and gazed down. For several moments, all I saw was the sheen of the water, gleaming like a black pearl. Then, quite suddenly, I could see the stars, as if the universe had flipped upside down, and the heavens blazed up from below the surface of the lake, rather than shining down from above.

Between one breath and the next, I thought. *That's how little time it takes to change perspective. The time it takes to count to five.*

"The waters of this lake can show many things," the Beast said quietly. "If you gaze into the water and wish hard enough, you may be offered a glimpse of what you wish for most."

"Can it show me my family?" I asked, gripping the gunwale tightly. *If I could just see them,* I thought. *Perhaps I would be less homesick. Perhaps I would find it easier to see what the Heartwood held inside.* "Can it show me my sisters, Papa, and Maman?"

"If that is what you truly wish for," the Beast replied.

I leaned out over the water, wishing with all my heart. As if in answer, the surface rippled. The stars seemed to blend together until the lake became filled with a hot, white light.

But I did not see my family. Instead, as if in a mirror, I saw two figures, a young man and a young woman, seated in a rowboat.

She was wearing a dark blue dress. He was clad in russet-colored velvet. As I watched, he leaned forward and held out a hand. She reached back. Their fingers touched. He carried her hand to his lips and pressed a kiss inside her palm.

No! I thought.

For I knew this couple. I had seen them on the gate, on the front door of the great stone house. Their images, their spirits, seemed to be everywhere on the Beast's lands. Until this moment, I had always assumed they were a couple from the past. A rendition of the young husband and wife buried beneath the Heartwood Tree.

But now, gazing down into the lake, I saw the truth in one great, blinding flash. This couple was the future of this place. Its salvation, not its past. What I had seen was still to come. All of a sudden, I was on my feet, heedless to the boat's rocking.

"Belle!" the Beast said sharply. "Sit down."

"Why did it show me that?" I gasped out. "That wasn't what I asked for."

"It must have been, at least in part. For the water shows only what the heart wishes, and when it does this, it cannot lie. That is the heart's true strength, the way it keeps us alive."

"But I don't want those images to be there. That isn't what I want!" I cried.

I tried to back away from him.

"Belle," he said again, urgently. "You must stop moving. You will overturn us both."

He reached up to steady me, but I jerked away from his outstretched hand and tumbled over the side.

The water closed over my head—cold, so very cold. I kicked my legs, desperately trying to get back to the surface, but my long skirts pulled me down and down. I opened my mouth, as if to scream in anguish and fear, and felt the cold kiss of the water against my tongue.

I am going to die, I thought.

But, suddenly, the Beast was there, his strong fingers closing over the hand I'd snatched away from him just moments before. He gave a great yank and my body shot upward. I was flying through the water now. The lights of the stars seemed to shimmer all around me. Then the world went black and I saw nothing more.

When I knew myself again I was lying sideways, cradled in a pair of impossibly strong arms. From a great distance, a voice was speaking—calling my name, begging me to answer, and cursing me, all at once. I pulled one aching breath into my lungs, gave way to a great bout of coughing, then tried again.

"Stop shouting," I managed to croak. "You're hurting my eardrums."

He made a sound then, the most human I'd ever heard him utter save for speech itself, something caught between laughter and a sob.

"For the love of God, what were you thinking, Annabelle?"

"It's no use scolding me," I said.

My stomach was full of jitters and my head felt light. I

wanted to lean my head against his shoulder and leave it there forever; I wanted to claw my way out of his arms.

"I'm sorry about the dress," I said.

He stopped walking. "I don't care about the dress and you know it." He gave me a shake, as if to rattle some sense into me. "Look at me. *Look at me, Annabelle.*"

"I can't!" I cried. "I don't know how. Stop acting like a Beast. Stop asking me to try."

He set me down, releasing me so abruptly the soles of my feet sang with pain as they hit the cobblestones. We were back at the house, in the courtyard. I had no idea we'd come so far, that he'd held me so long in his arms.

"Find what the Heartwood holds soon," he said.

Then he was gone.

Twenty-One

I SLEPT BADLY, MY DREAMS FULL OF WATER, AND AWOKE TO a sky filled with dark and glowering clouds. The air was as thick as damp cotton. I threw back the covers and got out of bed, leaving the bedclothes in a snarl. The change in the weather made me angry somehow, as if it, too, conveyed the Beast's displeasure, and kept me confined indoors.

We'll just see about that, I thought. Ignoring the wardrobe with its selection of fine dresses, I put on my plain homespun once more. Then I set out for the stables in search of Corbeau. I might not be able to do anything about the weather, but I definitely wasn't going to let it, or anything else, boss me around.

Fortunately for the success of my rebellion, Corbeau was in

his stall. This wasn't always the case. Sometimes the horse simply roamed free, other times the Beast rode him himself. Corbeau swiveled his head around as I came into the stall.

"Good morning," I crooned, running my fingers through his mane. "You'd like to go for a run, wouldn't you? You don't want to stay indoors any more than I do, do you, Corbeau?"

The horse whooshed out a breath, whether in agreement or disparagement of my proposed plan of action, I couldn't tell. But he made no objection as I saddled him and led him into the courtyard. I walked over to a stone planter flanking the steps to the house, clambered up it, and mounted Corbeau. As I settled into the saddle, he pranced a little, reaching out with his neck to feel the bit between his teeth.

"Take me somewhere, Corbeau," I commanded. "I don't care where, so long as it's away from here. Now run. *Run!*"

He shot from the courtyard like a bullet, heading for the orchard. Up and down the rolling land between the hills we went, as if running an obstacle course, then through a great meadow that lay beyond. The horse's coat grew shiny with sweat. My hair tumbled loose around my shoulders, curling in every direction as if each strand had a mind of its own. But no matter how far Corbeau and I ran together, I could not outrun the fact that I was trapped. I could no longer see the loveliness of the land all around me. All I saw were prison bars.

At last even Corbeau's strong legs grew tired, and his pace slowed. We settled into a walk, traveling aimlessly. Movement was all that was important. For once I stopped, I would be admitting the truth, admitting defeat: There was nowhere for me to go.

When I saw a pair of iron gates up ahead, I realized we had come to a place I recognized. It was the entrance to the Beast's lands, the same gate I'd passed through I had no idea how many days ago now.

I brought Corbeau to a halt, tossed my leg over his head and slid down. I caressed the black velvet of his nose. Ten steps took me to the gate. It was shut fast, the couple's hands clasped together tightly.

I moved forward until I stood before the image of the woman. *Let go,* I thought. *Let go of his hand and let me out.*

I felt a sob rise up, straight from my heart.

"Let me go," I said. I slammed my fist against the gate, felt the iron bite into my skin. "Let me go. Let me out."

Over and over I cried out my request, beating against the gate until my hands were bloody and raw. And still, the woman and her love clasped hands, pledging their devotion and my imprisonment both. Until at last, I sank to my knees, cradling my torn hands in my lap. Corbeau walked over to nuzzle the top of my head.

"Ah, Belle," I heard the Beast say behind me, so gently that it made me want to weep. "What have you done?"

"Go away," I said, without turning around. "I don't want to talk to you. I don't want to try, and fail, to gaze into your eyes. I don't need to be reminded that I can't see what's hidden in the

Heartwood, that I'm failing at the only thing I ever did well.

"I don't want to be here. I never wanted to be here. I want to go home."

A great stillness filled the air, as if the very land around me held its breath.

"Is that truly what you wish?" the Beast asked.

I did begin to weep then, great scalding tears, as the sob that rose from my heart threatened to split it open wide.

"Yes," I choked out. "I can't do what you need me to. I can't do anything right. I don't know why you even want to keep me here."

"Do you not?" the Beast asked quietly.

But by now I was weeping too hard to speak.

"Very well, then, Annabelle Evangeline Delaurier," he said. "I will not hold you here against your will. I will let you go."

I staggered to my feet. "Wait," I said, frantically wiping tears from my face with the backs of my hands. "Don't go like that, I . . . I don't understand why you're doing this. I haven't done anything you wanted."

"You came in the first place," he said. "Apparently, that must be enough. You should take Corbeau. He will speed your journey. If you hurry, you can be home by lunchtime."

"But you—what will happen to you?" I asked.

The Beast spun around so suddenly I faltered back a step, crashing against the gates. With a scream like an animal caught in a trap, they began to swing apart.

"I am finished answering your questions," he snarled. Never had he seemed more like a Beast than he did at this moment. "You asked to go; I have given you leave. I suggest you depart, before I change my mind."

He gave Corbeau a slap on the rump. The horse gave a cry, echoing that of the gate, and bolted forward. I stumbled after him. As I passed through the gate, I saw it had changed. It was broken, rusted. The couple's hands, once so tightly bound together, were shattered at the wrists. No longer would they be able to cling together. They were torn apart forever.

And it was only then that I realized I had left behind the branch of the Heartwood.

Twenty-Two

JUST AS THE BEAST PROMISED, I WAS HOME BY LUNCHTIME. Corbeau had halted not far from the gate. I hauled myself up onto his back, which took some doing as there was nothing to help me mount and my hands were raw. There was no chit-chat between me and the horse as we traveled this time. Before, Corbeau's gait had seemed even and smooth. Now it seemed likely to shake me apart, finding every loose stone or rut.

"I'm sorry," I finally said. "I'm sorry. I didn't mean to hurt him. I didn't know I could. I just wanted to see my family. Why is that so much to ask?"

Corbeau shook his head, as if to drive the sound of my voice from his ears, and kept walking. It didn't take long to leave the Wood behind. We reached the turnoff to the house, my house, just as the sun reached the top of the sky. I reined Corbeau to a halt for a moment, gazing at the place I'd come to think of as home.

The roses I had planted before I'd left had new green leaves. At the side of the house, I could see that April had hung a load of washing out to dry. As I watched, a figure appeared in the kitchen doorway, then came down the steps.

Papa! I thought.

I urged the horse forward then, banging my heels against his sides until at last he gave in and took me where I wanted to go. I saw my father lift a hand to shade his eyes, heard him give a great shout. And then I was in the yard with my family all around me.

I had done it. I was home.

"I still can't believe that Beast let you leave," Maman said several days later, for what felt like at least the millionth time.

I was putting away the clean dinner dishes. April and Dominic had gone for a walk. Celeste was visiting Corbeau in the stables to see if she could interest him in a carrot. The two had taken an unmistakable shine to each other. Papa was working on a project in his workshop. He'd spent more time in the workshop than he had in the house since I went away, according to Maman.

The days following my return had brought the color back

into my father's face, the straightness to his shoulders, though it had not quite erased the worry in his eyes. As for my mother, she had stayed by my side almost constantly, as if I might disappear or set off again if she didn't keep me in sight at all times.

By mutual, and silent, consent, once the general exclamation over my unexpected reappearance had died down, no one questioned me much about what my life had been like during the time that I was gone. It was as if we all wished to simply savor being together again. The explanations could wait, and they would come. Not that I had very satisfactory ones to give. For now, it was enough just to be at home.

"And I can't understand *why* he did it," my mother went on. "Why force you to come, then let you go before you'd accomplished what he wanted?"

I'm not so sure I understand, myself, I thought. Aloud, I gave the only explanation I had.

"He let me go because I asked him to, Maman."

My mother exhaled a quick breath through her nose. "Then you should have asked him to do it earlier," she said. "You would have saved us all a lot of worry, especially your Papa."

"I did," I said, suddenly remembering this. "It was almost the first thing I did ask for, in fact. He said no."

"Then why did he say yes the second time you asked?" my mother said.

"I don't know, Maman," I answered.

I don't know.

* * *

Grand-père Alphonse came to find me not long after. He had ridden from town just that morning to bring the news that the last of my father's ships had come safely to port. We were rich again. We could return to our old lives at any time we chose, if that was what we wanted.

Surprising as this news was, there was more to follow, for neither my mother nor my sisters, once so fashionable, seemed at all eager to get back to town. April and Dominic were planning to be married before he went back to sea in a ceremony that would take place beside the vegetable garden. They didn't seem the least bit interested in trading a simple country wedding for a fancier one in town.

We learned to be happy here, to be a true family, I thought. And happiness, once found, is hard to give up.

"Come take a walk with me, Belle," Grand-père Alphonse suggested as I finished the last of the washing-up chores. "We have a few moments of real daylight left before the sun goes down."

Twilight, I thought. I turned to my mother. "Would you like to come with us, Maman?"

"No, no, you go ahead," my mother said with a wave of her hand. "I have some sewing I want to do." My mother was embroidering the bodice of April's wedding dress.

Grand-père Alphonse and I went outdoors together, turning our footsteps toward the stream that ran behind the house.

"I have been watching you all day, Belle," Grand-père Alphonse observed after several minutes had gone by. "You are very quiet, and it seems to me that you are not quite yourself. Are you unhappy?"

"I shouldn't be," I said at once, as much to myself as to him, I think. "I got everything I wanted, didn't I?"

"I don't know. Did you?" asked Grand-père Alphonse.

"Of course I did," I replied. "I got to come home. The Beast let me go before he had to. I'm still not sure I understand why."

"Is that so?"

"Stop playing twenty questions with me, Grand-père Alphonse," I snapped. I stopped walking and gave a strangled laugh. "Oh, for heaven's sake. Now I sound just like him."

In the time I had been gone, Papa had built a bench to sit beside the stream. Grand-père Alphonse led me to it and we sat down.

"Tell me what distresses you so, *ma Belle*."

"I couldn't read the Heartwood, Grand-père Alphonse," I said. "I couldn't see its face, no matter how hard I tried. I failed him, and I'm so afraid . . ."

I broke off, battling a sudden impulse to weep.

"I'm so afraid I've failed us both somehow." I dashed a hand across one cheek, as the tears won the day and began to fall anyhow. I really *was* upset, much more than I had realized. "I hate to cry."

"I know you do," Grand-père Alphonse observed with a

gentle smile. He dug in his pants pocket and produced a hand-kerchief. "You always did, even as a child. Tell me more. What about him?"

"He's a Beast," I said, and blew my nose loudly. "What else is there to know?"

"There must be something, I think," Grand-père Alphonse said. "Or you would not be twisting my second-best hand-kerchief up into knots."

"He confuses me," I burst out. "He makes me confuse myself. One minute, he's asking for the impossible and all I want to do is run away. The next, all I want to do is give him what he wants."

"But surely you should only do that if it's what you want as well."

"I don't know what I want!" I wailed. "Can't you see that's the problem?"

Grand-père Alphonse opened his arms and enfolded me inside them. I wept as though the end of the world had come. He held me quietly until the storm had passed.

"I've ruined your shirt," I said after many moments.

"I doubt that," Grand-père Alphonse said mildly. "And even if you have, I have others." He ran a hand over my head, the way he did when I was a child. "May I tell you what I think, Belle?"

"I wish you would," I said.

"I think you do know what you want. The problem is you don't want to admit it."

I gave another sob, but I sat up. "I can't admit it," I said. "It's admitting the impossible. I'm not sure how long the Beast—I don't have anything else to call him but that—and I have actually known each other. I'm not even sure I like him. So how can it be that now that I'm away from him I find . . ."

I paused and pulled in one shaking breath. "How can it be that I love him? I don't even know when it happened. I wasn't even sure it had."

"It doesn't take very long," Grand-père Alphonse said. "As little as between one heartbeat and the next. Love is many things, *ma Belle*. And the face it wears is not always what we expect. That's one of the things that makes it wonderful."

"I've never seen his face," I said. "He's never seen mine. That's part of the problem."

"You think so?" Grand-père Alphonse asked. "I grant you seeing his face may be necessary to free him. Both you and your father have told us so. But it seems to me that a face is not required for the rest. For what love truly is, where it truly resides, is in a place that none of us can see."

"The heart," I whispered.

"Just so," said Grand-père Alphonse.

So I had seen a true vision in the lake that night, I thought. For I had wished to see what I loved most. And the lake had shown me the Beast and me together. But my eyes had not understood the image my heart rendered at my own request, for I had not yet learned to look with the eyes of love, the eyes of the heart.

I lifted my right hand and turned it over to gaze down into the palm, at the place where the young man in the vision had pressed his lips. I felt a fine tingling begin there, spreading out toward my fingertips, up my arm. It was the same sensation I experienced when a piece of wood began to share its secrets. The sensation the Heartwood had denied me for what felt like days without end, save for one moment only. The one in which the Beast and I had held it together.

"Oh, of course," I said aloud.

"Belle?" Grand-père Alphonse said.

"The Heartwood," I replied. "I tried so hard to see what it held within it, to find the face of true love. And all the time, I was going about it the wrong way. Looking for the wrong thing.

"It took two," I said. "Two different people to make the Heartwood what it is. Two different experiences, grief and joy, combined. True love never has just one face, does it? It must always have two, or it isn't true love at all.

"That's why I couldn't see anything, no matter how hard I looked. I was only looking for one thing, one face. I forgot that, to find true love, you must look with love's eyes."

"I think," Grand-père Alphonse said, "that you have grown very wise all of a sudden, *ma petite Belle*. What will you do with such wisdom, I wonder?"

"Go back," I answered at once. "He let me go because he loved me. I see that now. He gave me what I wanted most. He let me leave him. Now I have to go back and finish what I started. But first I must talk to Papa."

I stood up and started for the barn.

"You are sure, Belle?" my father asked a short time later. Following my startling pronouncement in his workshop, Papa had insisted we all go back to the house. Despite my sense of urgency, I had agreed. I had left my family once without saying good-bye. I would not do so a second time.

"As sure as I can be, Papa," I replied. "I think I understand"— I cast a quick look in Grand-père Alphonse's direction—"that I *see* the truth now. I understand why I could not read the Heartwood before."

"But you think you can now," my father said.

"Yes," I answered, just as I had in his workshop. "I do think so." I looked around, at my family's shocked and sober faces. "I can't leave this unfinished. It isn't right. But even more, going back is what is in my own heart."

"Well, then," my father said into the startled silence that greeted these words, "I think that you must follow your heart and go."

"Roger, how can you say such a thing?" my mother exclaimed. "How can you let her go into danger a second time?"

"I'm not so sure she's going into danger," my father said, his eyes on mine. There was not a trace of worry in them now. As if learning what I held in my heart had freed the pain he'd carried in his the whole time I'd been gone. "Perhaps she never was."

My father shifted his gaze to April, sitting at Dominic's side.

"I remember how April looked," he went on quietly, "when we did not know whether or not Dominic was coming home. Perhaps the greater danger lies in not finishing what is started, in carrying unanswerable questions all the days of our lives. And I think, finally, that I will put my trust in my daughter ahead of my own fear. I will put my trust in her strong heart."

"But he is a *Beast*," Maman protested, though I think even she knew that she had lost the argument.

"And Dominic was once a thief," April spoke up. "Not everyone ends the same as they begin, Maman. Papa is right. Belle's heart is strong. Give it the chance to find its own way. Let her go."

"Oh, very well, since I see I am outnumbered," my mother said waspishly, but I saw the sheen of tears in her eyes.

"Thank you," I said as I went to kiss her. I turned to face the rest of my family. "Thank you all."

And so I set out to find the heart of the Wood through no other enchantment than the strength of my will, with a power no greater than that which I carried in my heart.

I never would have made it, but for Corbeau. For it seemed to me that the Wood did not welcome me back. I had injured one it claimed as its own. The path turned and twisted where once it had run straight. Unexpected branches kept sweeping across it, as if to knock me from the back of the horse. A cold, sharp wind blew straight into my face, although it was early summer.

But Corbeau never faltered. I laced my fingers through his mane, closed my eyes, and held on tight. And so, throughout that long, cold night, I searched for the home of my beloved not with the eyes of the mind, but of the heart.

We came to the iron gates just at dawn.

The young woman still stood, one broken hand outstretched, but the right-hand side, the one with the image of the young man, had completely tumbled down. It lay in pieces on the ground. At the sight of it, a terrible fear seized my heart.

"Fly," I urged the horse. "Fly, Corbeau. Take me to him. Don't let me be too late."

Through the ruined gates and along the avenue, we flew, clattering up the hill and into the courtyard.

"I'm here. I've come back. Where are you?" I shouted. And it seemed my heart would break that I had never asked him for his name. I, who had been so very concerned about my own. But I would not call out for him, naming him a Beast.

I found him in the study.

He was sitting in a wingback chair, drawn up before the fireplace, the same one in which my father had fallen asleep, once upon a time. His long legs were stretched out before him. His head was thrown back. His eyes were closed. For one horrible, endless second, it seemed he did not breathe. Then I saw that he had the branch of the Heartwood clasped to his chest. In horror, I saw that the petals had begun to turn a color not a single one had ever been before: brown.

Oh, my love, I thought. *I came so close, so very close to losing you. To not seeing us both in time.*

I knelt down beside him, placed my hand on top of his hand where it clasped the Heartwood. The other I placed against his face, the one I'd tried so hard not to see for so very long.

"I want you to look at me," I said, willing it with all my might, with all my heart. "Open your eyes, and look into mine. I know you can hear me. I know you can do this.

"Please," I said. "Don't leave me, now that I've found you at last. Don't leave me to love alone."

I saw his eyelids flutter then. The power of the Heartwood sang up my arm. I felt his chest rise, as he pulled a single breath.

He opened his eyes, and looked straight into mine.

"One," I said, and watched his eyes widen.

"Two." His other hand came up, and covered mine.

"Three." The petals of the Heartwood flushed, as if they were a young girl blushing.

"Four." And now I could hardly see, for the tears that filled my eyes.

"Five."

There was a sound like a clap of thunder, the wings of wild birds, a single voice singing its favorite song on a clear, bright morning. The great stone house seemed to shake on its foundation. My gaze never faltered. I kept it steady on his, and realized that, at long last, I was seeing myself truly, reflected back through the eyes of true love.

I looked at him and saw a handsome young man with eyes of green and hair the color of copper.

"Tell me your name, if you please," I said. And, for the very first time, I saw him smile.

"Gaspard."

He sat up, then drew me into his lap, and pressed his lips to mine. I felt my heart beat, five deep strokes, and I knew that it was given to him for all time. Then Gaspard drew back and gazed into my face once more.

"I can see your eyes," he said, and his voice sounded just the same as it always had, heart and mind combined. And in it I heard more joy than I had ever believed possible.

"Your eyes are brown, Annabelle."

"Indeed they are," I said as my heart began the melody it would sing until the day it ceased to beat.

"And my name is Belle."

Twenty-Three

OUR STORY HAS A HAPPY ENDING, BUT THEN YOU'VE probably known that all along.

I gave Gaspard the Heartwood as a wedding present, for it finally revealed the secret it had guarded for so long. The face of true love, which is, of course, not one face at all but two, for true love cannot happen on its own. This was what I'd been missing, the piece of the puzzle you'd think would jump right out, but is, instead, the last one you find.

True love always takes two, for it is about another more than you yourself.

The two of us were married not long after April and Dominic. Like them, we clasped hands and said our vows standing beside the vegetable garden. There wasn't time to make me a dress as fine as April's. But Maman gave me her favorite silk shawl. April wove a wreath of roses for my hair. Celeste baked a cake so tall it almost failed to come out of the oven door. I walked toward my true love with my father on one side of me and Grand-père Alphonse on the other. And so, surrounded by all I loved, we spoke our vows.

Afterward, Gaspard and Dominic carried the kitchen trestle table out of doors, and, beside the stream that ran behind the house, we ate the wedding feast Celeste had prepared. And it was here that Gaspard presented to me the only wedding gift that I had asked for: his story.

"I'd like to be able to tell you that I was once someone important," he began. "A king or a prince, perhaps. But I was not, though my family was a noble one. We lived in the town by the sea, the same town you came from, sir," he said, turning to my father.

When I had first brought Gaspard home, he had immediately gone down on one knee before my father. There he'd asked both his forgiveness for the way he'd behaved in the Wood, and Papa's permission to marry his daughter. My father had given both.

"All my life, I had heard tales of the Wood," Gaspard went on. "Tales of its enchantment, tales of its power, which was said to be that of life itself. It was for these reasons that we did no hunting there, in spite of the game that was abundant. It was said that your eyes could deceive you within the boundaries of the Wood, for only those whose own hearts were true could see what lived there in their own true forms.

"And if you did not see truly yet took what the Wood did not wish to give, then its power would exact a terrible price."

"No one hunts there even today," my father said. "Though the reason you give has been lost over the years."

"How long were you in the Wood?" Dominic asked quietly.

"I'm not certain," Gaspard replied. "A very long time, I think. So long a time I knew no way to count it."

"But why?" I asked.

He gave my hand a squeeze. "As punishment. For, in the arrogance of youth, I decided that the rules need not apply to me. This, in spite of the fact that my heart was far from true, for obviously it was filled with my own desires alone. One day, I shot and killed a doe. I did not know—I did not see—that she had a fawn. The grief of the child for its mother was piteous to see. Even I came to regret what I had done.

"This was the only thing that saved me, in the end, I think. The reason the power of the Wood let me live instead of simply claiming my life as payment for the doe's. She rose up before me, and as she did, her form changed, and she became the loveliest young woman I had ever beheld. She gathered the fawn up into her arms.

"'See the grief your thoughtless act has caused?' she asked, the tears hot upon her cheeks. 'Since you behave no better than a beast, you may wear the form of one. Since you refuse to use your heart to see, your eyesight will be clouded. That which pains you will be easy to see. That which you desire most will be hidden from you.

"'And this is how you will remain until the day that one true heart, with eyes to match, finds the way to free you from this curse you now bring upon yourself.'"

"That's why you wanted to know what the Heartwood held," I said. "For no eyes see more truly than those of true love."

"As you have demonstrated," he said with a smile.

"As we *both* have demonstrated," I replied.

"Oh, for heaven's sake," Celeste exclaimed. "Between the two of you and April and Dominic, all this lovey-dovey carrying on is enough to turn my stomach."

By which you can see that not everything about us had changed. Celeste still had her sharp mind and equally sharp tongue. Today, however, she also had a twinkle in her eyes.

I laughed. "You only say that because you're the oldest," I replied. "You were supposed to get married first."

Celeste shook her head with a smile. "I am finished with the way things are supposed to be," she said. "And so, I think, we all are. No matter what the rest of you decide to do, I'm staying here. I like the country."

"But you can't stay on your own," I protested. Papa and Maman had already announced their intention to return to the city, at least for a while.

"She won't be alone," April said. "I'll stay with her, at least until Dominic comes back from sea."

"I was hoping you'd say that," Celeste said. "Without you, I'd have to do the dishes myself."

"But what about when he comes back?" I asked.

Celeste reached across the table to take my hand. "Do not worry about me, *ma petite Belle*. You and April found your way, and I am happy for you both. Now you must let me find mine. But you and Gaspard—what will you do?"

"We will go back to the great stone house in the Wood," I replied. "There is a story there—more than one, I think— which I would like to understand before we settle anywhere else. And there is the Heartwood, too."

"Come to us at Christmas, all of you," Gaspard proposed. "And we will make the house that was so long a place of loneliness one of joy."

And so, after many days together and of making preparations, those of us who would make the journey through the Wood were ready to go. April stayed behind with Celeste. Papa, Maman, along with Grand-père Alphonse, Gaspard, and I set out. The path through the Wood ran as straight as ever, save for the narrow, winding path that curved into its very heart. There was no way to miss it now.

Gaspard and I parted from my family, and rode to the great stone house in silence, with me seated before him on Corbeau. The iron gates stood open, as if welcoming us home. Every tree in the orchard was in bloom, though the days were shortening now. We left Corbeau in his stable. Then, hand in hand, we walked to where the Heartwood stood by the shore of the lake.

"Look," I said when I saw it. "Oh, look, Gaspard."

The blossoms of the Heartwood tree lay scattered on the ground. But in their place, its boughs were filled with fruit as ripe and golden as the sun. Slowly, almost reverently, I moved to lay a hand against the bark.

"Someday," I said softly, "this tree will die. But what it carried in its heart will never be extinguished. Its roots go too deep, the fruit it bears is too nourishing, and the promise carried on the scent of its blossoms travels too far.

"True love may not always be easy to see, but once it has been discovered it can never be lost."

"You are as honest at the end as you were at the beginning," my true love said.

And I put my arms around him and kissed him beneath the branches of the Heartwood Tree, feeling my heart ache at the pure joy.